Dear Reader,

I just wanted to t̶___ ___ ___ ___ ___ ___ ___t
my publisher has ___ ___ ___ ___ ___ ___y
earlier books. Some ___ ___ have not been available
for a while, and amongst them there are titles that
have often been requested.

I can't remember a time when I haven't written,
although it was not until my daughter was born that
I felt confident enough to attempt to get anything
published. With my husband's encouragement, my
first book was accepted, and since then there have
been over 130 more.

Not that the thrill of having a book published gets
any less. I still feel the same excitement when a new
manuscript is accepted. But it's you, my readers, to
whom I owe so much. Your support—and particularly your letters—give me so much pleasure.

I hope you enjoy this collection of some of my
favourite novels.

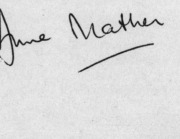

Back by Popular Demand

With a phenomenal one hundred and thirty books published by Mills & Boon, Anne Mather is one of the world's most popular romance authors. Mills & Boon are proud to bring back many of these highly sought-after novels in a special collector's edition.

ANNE MATHER: COLLECTOR'S EDITION

SANDSTORM

BY
ANNE MATHER

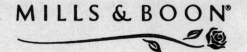

MILLS & BOON®

*All the characters in this book have no existence outside the imagina-
tion of the author, and have no relation whatsoever to anyone bearing
the same name or names. They are not even distantly inspired by any
individual known or unknown to the author, and all the incidents are
pure invention.*

*MILLS & BOON and MILLS & BOON with the Rose Device
are registered trademarks of the publisher.*

*First published in Great Britain 1980 by Mills & Boon Limited
This edition 1998
Harlequin Mills & Boon Limited,
Eton House, 18-24 Paradise Road, Richmond, Surrey TW9 1SR*

© Anne Mather 1980

ISBN 0 263 80561 1

*Set in Times Roman 11 on 11½ pt by
Rowland Phototypesetting Limited
Bury St Edmunds, Suffolk*

74-9801-50862

*Made and printed in Great Britain by
Caledonian International Book Manufacturing Ltd, Glasgow*

CHAPTER ONE

ABBY stood behind the kitchen door, with her hands pressed hard against her burning cheeks. She hoped no one had observed her hasty departure from the party, or if they had, that they assumed she was helping Liz with the washing up. The last thing she wanted was to draw attention to herself, and at least in the kitchen she could not be seen.

Dry-mouthed, she moved away from the door, glad that the caterers who had been here earlier had departed some time ago. It would have been awkward, explaining her withdrawal from the proceedings to them, and she supposed she ought to be grateful there was no one to witness her consternation. But how could she have anticipated that Rachid would turn up here, at Liz's party, when she had not even known he was in London?

Taking long gulping intakes of air, she endeavoured to calm herself. It was ridiculous behaving like this, she told herself impatiently. She was a grown woman, not a child. She should be capable of handling any situation, including meeting the husband she had not seen for almost eighteen months. She was Brad's secretary, wasn't she? The cool collected recipient of his confidences, and no longer the wide-eyed innocent she had been when she first met Rachid. At just such a party as this, she thought bitterly—only in Paris, not at her friend's apartment in London.

Liz!

With a puzzled frown she considered the possibility that Liz had known Rachid might appear. Liz knew everyone, and her job at the news agency ensured that she knew most of what they were doing as well. It was inconceivable that she should not have learned that the son of an eminent Middle Eastern prince was in town, so why hadn't she told Abby? The answer was obvious. Because if Abby had suspected her husband might be here, she herself would not have come.

Nibbling at her lower lip, Abby braced herself against the sink. She supposed it had been bound to happen sooner or later, that she should meet Rachid again, if not socially then at least commercially. Since she had taken up the post of Brad's secretary once more, her work brought her into contact with the oil barons of the world, and after all, it was through Brad that she had met Rachid in the first place.

But Liz! She and Liz had been friends since schooldays. She had known how she felt. Had known that she had no desire to meet her husband again—not yet. It was too soon. And she half wished she had not succumbed to her father's pleas to her to return to England. Without his entreating letters, she would still be working at the trade mission in New York, and she felt a surge of frustration that she should have allowed herself to be persuaded to take up her old life.

And yet, she argued logically, couldn't this have happened just as easily in New York?

Rachid was not bound by the conventions and limitations which had restricted his ancestors. He was a man of the twentieth century. He flew all over the world on business for his father. He looked like a European, and he dressed like a European, and only in his own country did he shed the trappings of the Western world.

Nevertheless, Abby knew that the chances of her encountering Rachid in New York had to be less likely. Her work there had not afforded her the same opportunities she had as Brad's secretary, and besides, so far as she knew, Rachid did not know where she was. All correspondence between them had been through her father's house in London, and he had distinct orders not to give her address to anyone without first consulting her.

The door behind her opened and she swung round apprehensively, half afraid that Rachid had seen where she had gone and followed her. But it was Liz Forster who came into the room, viewing her friend with wry knowing eyes. She was a tall girl, about Abby's height of five feet seven inches, with narrow bones and slightly angular features. She did not have Abby's smoothness or roundness, for although Abby was slim—too slim, her father thought—she retained a lissom grace, that was evident in the curve of her hips and the fullness of her breasts.

Now Liz closed the door behind her, and leaning back against it, folded her arms. 'Don't tell me,' she said, as Abby's lips parted in involuntary protest. 'You've seen him!' She shook her head. 'Is that why you're skulking out here?'

'I am not skulking,' declared Abby, straightening up from the sink, and rubbing her chilled palms together. 'I am merely trying to decide why you should do such a thing.'

Liz sighed, pushing herself away from the door. 'You're angry,' she said flatly.

'Did you expect anything else?'

Liz shrugged. 'I suppose not.'

Abby gazed at her helplessly. 'Liz, you must have known how I would react. That's why you didn't tell me, isn't it? Why you let me stand there like a lemon, when Damon brought him in.'

'Did he see you?'

'No.' Abby pressed her lips together. 'At least, I don't think he did. You can never be absolutely sure with Rachid. He has the eyes of a hawk!'

'A desert hawk,' replied Liz dryly. Then: 'I'm sorry, Abby, but I had to do it.'

'Why? Why did you have to?' Abby could not accept that. 'You could have warned me, at least.'

'And then you wouldn't have come,' Liz exclaimed, reminding her of her own words. 'Abby, does it really matter? I mean, you have to meet him some time, don't you? Even if it's only in the divorce court.'

Abby's lips thinned. 'Don't you know?' she taunted bitterly. 'Muslims don't have to do anything so boringly official. All Rachid has to do is say the words of repudiation and he's a free man. Besides, why should he do that? He's allowed four wives anyway.'

'Abby!' Liz came towards her, putting a sympathetic hand on her shoulder. 'Rachid's a Christian. You told me so yourself—'

'Is he?' Abby moved away from her.

'Abby, you know—'

'I'd really rather not talk about it, Liz.' She moved her head jerkily, feeling the weight of her hair heavy at her nape. 'And if you don't mind, I'd like to leave—as soon as possible. Would you get my coat? It's in the bedroom. I'll just slip out the back way—'

'Speak to him, at least,' Liz protested, appalled. 'What's the matter? You're surely not afraid of him, are you? Heavens, you were married for almost three years! Doesn't that entitle him to five minutes of your time?'

Abby's eyes blazed. 'Rachid's entitled to nothing from me, nothing!' she declared fiercely. 'I don't know what kind of moral blackmail he used on you to get you to invite him here—'

'Damon asked if he could bring a friend,' retorted Liz crossly. Damon Hunter was her boss at the agency. 'How did I know—'

'You mean, you didn't?' Abby looked at her sceptically, and even Liz could not sustain that challenging gaze.

'Oh, all right,' she said, picking up a canapé from a half empty tray and biting into it delicately. 'Damon told me who it was. But I didn't know you were going to throw a fit of hysterics, did I?'

Abby bent her head. 'Will you get my coat?'

'Abby, please—'

Liz looked at her imploringly, and Abby heaved a sigh. 'I can't stay here,' she said firmly. 'I'm not hysterical, and I'm not afraid of seeing Rachid again, I just—don't want to—to speak to him.'

Liz shook her head. 'Damon's going to be furious!'

'Damon is?' Abby was confused.

'Yes.' Liz moved her shoulders awkwardly. 'Oh, if you must know, he asked me to give this party, to invite you here. Rachid—'

'You mean Rachid arranged it?' Abby demanded angrily. 'Oh, Liz, how could you?'

Liz grimaced. 'I didn't have much choice, did I? Damon is my boss!'

Abby clenched her fists. 'I won't do it, Liz. I won't!'

'All right, all right.' Liz made a deprecatory gesture. 'No one can force you.'

'No.' But Abby was not completely convinced. She knew her husband. She knew his capacity for coercion and for the first time she wondered why he particularly wanted to see her now, just when she was beginning to feel secure once more.

'I'll get your coat,' said Liz suddenly, walking towards the door. 'You wait here. I won't be long.'

'And if Damon—'

'Leave it to me,' replied Liz quietly, and Abby fretted uneasily until she came back again, carrying the pigskin coat that Abby had arrived in. 'Here you are,' she said, helping her on with it. 'You can leave by the service door. There's no lift, I'm afraid, but the stairs will bring you out on to Gresham Place.'

'Thanks.' Abby curled the soft fur collar up about her ears, its darkness complementing her extreme fairness. 'I'm sorry about this, Liz, but I can't face Rachid. Not tonight.'

Liz shrugged. 'If you say so.'

'You do understand, don't you?'

Liz hesitated. 'Not entirely.' She paused, and then seeing Abby's anxious expression, she went on: 'Darling, Rachid's a dish, in anyone's vocabulary. I could never understand why not having a baby meant that much to you. I mean—heaps of couples—'

Abby moved towards the service door. 'You're right, Liz,' she said tightly. 'You don't understand. Anyway. . .' she made an awkward movement of her shoulders, 'I must go. Goodnight, and—and thank you.'

'I'll ring you next week,' said Liz, following her to the door, and Abby nodded.

'Yes, do that,' she agreed, and with a faint smile she let herself out on to the concrete hallway that gave access to the rear of the flats.

Liz's flat was on the seventh floor, and Abby was relieved when she finally reached the door on to the street. Fourteen flights of stairs had seemed interminable, and she expelled her breath weakly as she emerged from the building.

It was a chilly October evening, with a thin mist rising from the river. Drifts of fallen leaves choked the gutters, and Abby pushed her hands into her pockets as she stepped out along the pavement towards Gresham Square. She might find a taxi outside the apartments, she decided hopefully, eager to put as much distance between her and Rachid as she could in the shortest possible time.

She was completely unaware of being observed, so that when the tall figure stepped in front of her, she thought for a moment that she was being accosted. Her breath escaped on a trembling gasp and she lifted her head in anxious protest, only to step back aghast when she encountered the dark impassioned gaze of her husband. In spite of what had gone before, he was the last person she had expected to meet out here, and it was only as she took another backward step that she realised he was not alone. Two men had silently paced her progress along the street, and this meeting with Rachid was no coincidence, but a well-executed ambush. Oh, *Liz*, she thought despairingly, how could you? How could you?

'Good evening, Abby.'

Rachid's voice was rich and dark and smooth, like a fine wine, she thought imaginatively, belying the controlled anger she had glimpsed in the shadowy depths of his eyes. He spoke with scarcely a trace of an accent, but that was hardly surprising considering he had been educated at the most exclusive establishments England had to offer, and what was more to the point, his grandmother *was* English. He stood looking down at her, for although she was a tall girl, he still topped her by a few inches, waiting for her reply, and with a feeling of impotence bordering on the hysteria Liz had hinted at earlier, Abby inclined her head.

'Good evening, Rachid.'

A snap of his fingers sent his two henchmen several yards along the street, and then, in the same controlled tones, he continued: 'You refused to speak to me at the home of your friend.

I regret this—er—stratagem, but I was determined that we should talk, Abby.'

Abby's hands balled in her pockets, but she
managed to hold up her head. At least in the
shadowy illumination of the street lamps he was
unable to see the anxious colour that had filled
her cheeks, or the unsteady quiver of her lips,
and forcing a note of indifference, she said:

'You could have telephoned me. If not at home,
then at the office. I presume you do know I've
gone back to work for Brad Daley. I'm sure
your—spies have been at their work.'

'Spies!' His tongue flicked the word contemptuously. Then, as if impatient with this
unsatisfactory encounter, he gestured along the
street. 'Come, my car is parked nearby. Let me
escort you home. We can talk more comfortably
out of this damp atmosphere.'

Abby stood her ground. 'I really don't see what
we have to talk about, Rachid,' she insisted
firmly. 'I—well, I told Liz I didn't wish to speak
to you, and I thought she would respect my confidence. Just because she hasn't, I see no reason
to change my mind—'

'Elizabeth—Liz—had no opportunity to
respect your confidence,' he retorted shortly, narrow lines bracketing his mouth. 'When I realised
you were no longer in the apartment, I came after
you. It was reasonable that as you had not used
the lifts, you must perforce have used the stairs.'

Abbey felt a little of the sense of betrayal leave
her. 'It makes no difference—'

'It does to me,' Rachid thrust the hands he had
been holding behind his back into the pockets of

the dark overcoat he was wearing, glancing about him almost irritably. 'Abby, I did not come here to stand arguing with you in the street. Have the goodness to accompany me back to my car. I promise, I am not intent on abducting you without your consent. I merely wish us to—to talk.'

'What about?' Abby was suspicious.

'Allah give me strength!' Rachid half turned away from her. Why will you not do as I ask you? Just this once? Surely it is not so much to ask? You are still my wife, after all.'

'Am I?' Her brows arched.

'What do you mean?' He turned to look at her with dark intensity.

Abby shrugged, a little unnerved by his hard scrutiny. 'I thought—that is—you might have divorced—'

'Enough!' There was no mistaking the fact that he was angry now. 'You are my wife! And so you will remain. Now, will you come with me without protest, or must I ask Karim and Ahmed—'

Abby's eyes blazed. 'You'd do that? You'd forcibly make me go with you?'

'Be still, Abby.' He drew a heavy breath. 'This conversation is rapidly becoming ridiculous! Is it so unreasonable that having not laid eyes on you for almost two years—'

'Eighteen months.'

'—I might wish for a little speech with you?'

'I told you in my letters—'

'—that you did not wish to see me, yes, I know.' Rachid's breathing indicated his impatience. 'But I do not accept that. I have never accepted that. I waited—not patiently, I admit, but I waited even so, for you to come to your senses. When you did not, I came after you, only to find you were no longer in London.'

'When was that?' Abby was curious.

'I do not know exactly. Six months, maybe nine months ago. It seems much longer, but I cannot be sure.'

Abby shifted her weight from one foot to the other. 'You saw—my father?'

'Yes, I saw him.'

Abby frowned. 'He didn't tell me.'

'Would it have made any difference if he had?' Rachid moved his shoulders indifferently. 'He would not give me your address.'

Abby's lips twisted. 'No? And didn't you threaten him? Couldn't you blackmail him into doing as you wanted?'

Rachid's features hardened. 'You have a viper's tongue, Abby. I had forgotten that.'

The mildly spoken comment infuriated her. Despite his anger, he was still able to control his speech, and her response was childishly vehement. 'Then no doubt you're well rid of me!' she taunted, only to break off abruptly when he possessed himself of her arm.

'Come,' he said, and the warning brilliance of his eyes silenced the protest that trembled on her lips.

Inwardly seething, she had no choice but to accompany him along the narrow street that opened into the square beyond. Karim and Ahmed moved obediently ahead, and by, the time Abby and Rachid turned the corner, the two men were already unlocking the doors of a sleek black limousine that awaited them. Like Rachid, they too were dressed in Western clothes, but whereas his features were arguably European, theirs were unquestionably Arab.

Rachid escorted Abby to the nearside door and when one of the men opened it, he propelled her inside. She panted briefly, in the aftermath of keeping up with his long-strided gait, and then hastily scrambled to the far side of the car as he climbed in after her. The two men took their seats in front, and the glass partition between successfully isolated them in a cocoon of supple leather and tinted glass.

The engine fired at the first attempt, and Abby sank back uneasily against the upholstery as the long Mercedes moved away. It was almost two years since she had ridden in such arrant luxury, and while resentment simmered at this unwanted encounter, her limbs responded to the sumptuous comfort of her surroundings.

But she was no longer seduced by such things. Time, and experience, had taught her that it was people and not possessions that ultimately governed one's life, that no inanimate object, no matter how extravagant, could compensate for disillusionment.

'You have been working in New York,' Rachid said now, half turning towards her on the cushioned seat, and Abby made a gesture of acknowledgement.

'I thought you didn't know where I was?' she countered, and he expelled his breath on a sound of impatience.

'Since your return to London, I have learned everything about you,' he retorted. 'Daley is not as secretive about his employees as you would obviously like. With the better half of a bottle of Scotch malt beneath his belt, he had few inhibitions.'

Abby pursed her lips. 'You mean—you pumped Brad?'

Rachid shook his head. 'Not me, personally, no. But I do have some friends.'

Abby felt a surge of indignation. 'You mean you have influence with people!' she asserted coldly. 'You use people, Rachid.' Her lips curled. 'You always did.'

Rachid's expression was hidden from her, but she sensed his heated reaction to the insult. Wives of Middle Eastern princes did not answer back, that much she had learned in her years in Abarein. At least, they hadn't, until she came on the scene. But she had been stupid enough to imagine she had been different, that she and Rachid had had a deeper relationship than those foolish acolytes who only hovered on the brink of their husband's notice.

'This conversation is getting us nowhere,' he said at last. 'I have been very patient, Abby, but now my patience is wearing thin. I want you back. I want you to return with me—to Xanthia.'

Abby choked. 'You're not serious!'

'But I am,' he assured her, in that calm, implacable tone. 'You are my wife, Abby, and as such you belong in my house. I do not intend that this situation should continue any longer. I need a wife—I need you. I expect you to adhere to my wishes.'

Abby felt a rising sense of incredulity that threatened to explode in hysterical laughter. He couldn't be serious, but he was! He actually expected her to give up the new life she had made for herself and return with him to Abarein, to the palace at Xanthia, which he shared with his father and the rest of his family.

Abby pushed forward on the seat and reached for the handle of the door. 'I think you're right,' she said, momentarily surprising him by what he thought was her submission. 'This conversation is getting us nowhere. If you'll ask your driver to stop here, I can take a bus—'

Rachid's utterance was not polite, and she turned startled eyes in his direction. 'You are not getting out of this car until I have the answer I seek,' he told her grimly, 'and I suggest you give the matter careful consideration before creating circumstances you will find hard to redeem.'

Abby gasped. 'You said you were not abducting me!' she burst out tremulously. 'And now you say—'

'For God's sake, you are my wife, Abby!' he overrode her harshly. 'How can I abduct my wife? You belong to me!'

'I belong to no one,' she retorted, her breathing quickening again. 'Rachid, you have no right—'

'I have every right. By the laws of your country and mine—'

'Laws!' Abby cast an anxious look through the windows of the limousine. 'Rachid, marriage is not governed by laws! It's governed by needs—

by emotions! And most of all, by trust.'

Rachid leant towards her. 'I trust you.'

'But I don't trust you!' she averred unsteadily. 'Rachid, can't you see you're wasting your time? Our—our marriage is over, as surely as if we had untied the knot ourselves.'

'I will not accept that.'

'You'll have to. I'm not coming back to you, Rachid. I—I don't love you.'

'I love you.'

'Do you?' Abby's mouth quivered. 'I'm afraid your ideas of love and mine are sadly different.'

Rachid's hand was suddenly hard upon her knee. 'Listen to me, Abby. I need you—'

'You need a woman,' Abby corrected tautly. 'Only a woman. Any woman—'

'No!'

'Yes.' She tried to dislodge those hard fingers which were digging into the bone. 'You only think you want me because I left you. When I was there. . .'

'Yes? When you were there? Did I not treat you as the much-loved wife of my father's eldest son?'

Abby bent her head. 'You treated me— honorably, yes. But you know as well as I do, that—that isn't enough.' She shook her head. 'Rachid, you know you must have an heir. And we both know that you're not to blame for not producing one.'

'*Abby*!'

His tone was impassioned now, and she knew she had lit some flame of remembrance inside him. It was hard for him, she knew that, but where there was no fidelity there was no trust, and she would not—she *could* not—share him with his mistresses.

'Abby,' he went on now, 'I know my father spoke with you—'

'You do?' She stiffened.

'Yes.' He uttered a harsh oath. 'Sweet mother of the Prophet, do you think I did not turn heaven and earth to find out why you had left without telling me?'

'You knew why I'd left,' she reminded him, as memories fanned the fires of her resentment. 'Your father's words were no news to me. You'd made the position quite clear enough.'

'Abby, listen to me. . .'

'No, you listen to me.' She succeeded in thrusting his long fingers aside and moved as far away from him as she could. 'When I married you, I was an innocent, I realise that now. I believed— I really believed you loved me—'

'I did. I *do*!'

She shook her head. 'I know that it was partly my fault. I know you were disappointed when we didn't have a child—'

'Abby!'

'—but these things happen, even in the best of families. There was nothing I could do.'

'I know that.'

'You should have divorced me then,' she went on in a low monotone. 'You should have set us both free. At least I would have been spared the humiliation of—of—and you could have married the—the wife your father chose for you.'

'Abby, I did not want the wife my father chose for me. I wanted you!'

'Not enough,' she said painfully. 'Oh, this is hopeless, Rachid. We're just going over all the old ground. Why couldn't you just have accepted that our marriage was over and freed yourself? I wouldn't have stood in your way—'

'Abby, stop this!'

'I won't. I can't. I did love you Rachid, once. But I don't love you now. And I won't come back to you.'

'Abby, you're my wife—'

'You'd have been better making me your mistress,' she retorted recklessly. 'Mistresses aren't expected to produce heirs. As it happens, I would have had to refuse that offer, but it would have saved us both a lot of heartache.'

Rachid took a deep breath. 'Abby, I don't care about an heir. For the love of God, listen to me! My father now knows how I feel. There will be no more of his philosophising—'

'No, there won't,' Abby interrupted him shortly. 'Because I'm not coming back, Rachid. You'll have to drug me or knock me unconscious to get me to go with you, and somehow I don't think the Crown Prince would like it to be known that his wife is so unwilling.'

Rachid's eyes glittered in the dim light. 'You will fight me?'

'Every inch of the way.'

He hesitated a moment, and then picked up the intercom that connected to his bodyguard in front. '26, Dacre Mews,' he directed shortly, giving the address of Abby's father's house, and then sank back against the soft leather at his side of the car, resting his head wearily against the window frame.

Abby's silently expelled sigh of relief was tinged with unexpected compassion. So, she thought weakly, he had accepted her arguments. He was taking her home; and while she was grateful for the victory, she wondered if she had really won. She had never known Rachid give up without a battle, and reluctant emotion stirred in the embers of discontentment. Once she would not have hesitated in giving in to him. Once he had controlled her every waking breath. But no longer. And although she was glad of the freedom, she remembered the sweetness of the past with unbearable bitterness.

Rachid let her out of the car in Dacre Mews, and waited, a tall, dark figure standing beside the limousine, as she fumbled for her key. It was only as she stumbled into the house that he climbed back into the vehicle, and she heard the whisper of its tyres as it moved away.

CHAPTER TWO

HER father was in his study. He looked up rather myopically as she put her head round the door, removing the thick-lensed spectacles to blink at her in surprise.

'You're early aren't you?' he asked, trying to focus on the dial of his pocket watch. 'I thought you were going to Liz's party.'

Abby tried to keep her tone light. 'I was. I did. I just came home sooner than I expected, that's all.'

'Why?' Professor Gillespie scratched his scalp through the thinning strands of grey hair. 'Wasn't it any good? I thought you usually enjoyed Liz's company.'

'I do, usually,' agreed Abby, withdrawing her head again, in two minds whether to mention Rachid to her father or not. 'I'm going to make some coffee,' she called. 'Do you want some?'

'I'd rather have cocoa at this time of the night,' replied her father absently. 'It's ten o'clock. I think I'll have a sandwich.'

'I'll make it,' Abby assured him, her voice drifting back to him as she walked into the kitchen.

The Gillespie house was one of a terrace, matching its fellows on either side. Tall and narrow, it stretched up three floors, with the kitchen, the dining room, and her father's study on the

23

ground floor, and living rooms and bedrooms above. It was easier for Professor Gillespie to work at ground level, even though it would have been quieter on the upper floors, but since his retirement from the University, her father had taken private students, and it was less arduous for him not to have stairs to negotiate every time he had to answer the door.

He came into the kitchen as Abby was spreading the bread with butter, filching a piece of cheese from the slices she had prepared. Although he was only in his early sixties, he looked older, and Abby knew he had aged considerably since her mother's death a year ago. Nevertheless, he enjoyed his work, and it had become both a pleasure and a distraction, filling the empty spaces he would otherwise have found unbearable.

Now he studied his daughter's bent head with thoughtful eyes, before saying perceptively: 'What's happened? Have you and Liz had a row or something? You're looking very flushed.'

Abby sighed, turning to the kettle that was starting to boil and lifting out earthenware beakers from the cupboard above. 'Oh, you know Liz,' she said, trying to sound inconsequent. 'She's not the type to row over anything. She's far too together for that.'

Professor Gillespie grimaced. 'Together!' he repeated distastefully. 'Where do young people find these words? Together means in company with someone else.'

'Well, she's usually that, too,' remarked Abby,

hoping to change the subject, but he was not to be diverted.

'Did something go wrong at the party?' he persisted, helping himself to a second wedge of cheese, and Abby was forced to accept that she was going to have to tell him the truth.

'Did—er—did you see Rachid while I was working in New York?' she asked carefully, and Professor Gillespie made a sound of resignation.

'You know, I half guessed that's what it might be,' he exclaimed, shaking his head. 'Come on, you might as well get it off your chest. Was Rachid at the party?'

Abby nodded. 'Liz's boss—Damon Hunter—he arranged it. I didn't know anything about it until I saw him coming in.' She moved her shoulders awkwardly. 'I got out of there as soon as I possibly could.'

'But not soon enough, obviously,' observed her father dryly. 'I gather you and Rachid had some conversation.'

'You could say that.' The kettle began to sing and she moved to make the cocoa. 'But not at the party. Rachid brought me home.'

'Did he?' Her father looked surprised, and Abby hastened to explain.

'He was waiting for me outside. He had two of his muscle men with him, so I couldn't exactly argue.'

Professor Gillespie sighed. 'I suppose he told you, he came to see me just after your mother died?'

Abby nodded. 'Why didn't you tell me?'

Her father grimaced. 'I didn't know what to

do. I didn't want to worry you. I mean, living in New York, away from all your friends and family—I thought it was unnecessary to alarm you.'

'I did make friends in New York, you know,' she pointed out quietly. 'But I know what you mean. If I'd known Rachid was looking for me, I'd probably have anticipated the worst.'

Professor Gillespie looked troubled. 'I thought about this for a long time before I asked you to come home,' he said thoughtfully. 'I knew if you came back to England, Rachid was bound to find out sooner or later, but I felt, rightly or wrongly, that with my backing he might hesitate before upsetting you. But he has upset you, hasn't he? I can see that. What does he want? A divorce?'

Abby's lips trembled, and she caught her lower lip between her teeth so that her father should not see that betraying sign. 'He wants me to go back to him,' she said flatly, avoiding his startled gaze. 'He said that was why he asked you for my address.'

Professor Gillespie sought one of the tall stools that flanked the narrow breakfast bar, and stared at her aghast. 'He wants to take you back to Abarein?'

'Yes.'

The Professor shook his head. 'But what about his father?'

'Rachid says that his father will accept me.'

'And are you going?'

Abby gave him the benefit of her violet gaze, her pupils wide and distended. 'Do you have to ask?'

Professor Gillespie looked more disturbed than ever. 'But Abby—'

'I didn't leave Rachid because of what his father said,' she retorted. 'At least, only in part. You know why I left, and that situation has not changed. Nor is it likely to do so.'

Her father cradled his chin on an anxious hand. 'I know, my dear, but have you really considered what you are refusing?'

Abby gasped. 'Do you want me to go back to him?'

'I want you to be happy,' her father insisted gently. 'You know that. And I also know that you love Rachid despite—'

'Loved, Dad, *loved*!' she contradicted him tightly. 'I did love him, you're right. I—I loved him very much. And I thought he loved me. But the Muslim way of loving is obviously different.'

'Abby, Rachid's a Christian, you know that. And besides, even if he were not, even if he embraced the faith of his ancestors, nowadays even kings and princes have only one wife at a time.'

Abby closed her eyes against the pain his words evoked. Even now, the remembrance of Rachid's treachery hurt, but that would pass. In time, everything passed; even hatred, which was all she felt for Rachid.

Opening her eyes again, she applied herself to the sandwiches. Then, sensing her father was waiting for a reply, she said: 'I have no intention of returning to Abarein, or to Rachid, for that matter. I made one mistake, but I don't intend to make another. Believe it or not, I like my work,

I like being independent, and while I appreciate your concern, Dad, I think I know what I want from life better than you do.'

'And what about later on? When you get older? When I'm dead and buried? What then?'

Abby sighed. 'There's always the possibility that I might get married again,' she said, handing him the plate of sandwiches. 'But whatever happens, it's my decision.'

Professor Gillespie took the plate, but he was still uneasy. 'Abby, men are not like women,' he insisted, as they walked back to the warm security of his study. 'Don't you think you're being a little unrealistic?'

Abby took a deep breath. 'I thought you were supposed to be on my side.'

'I am, I am.' Her father sought the comfort of his armchair with a troubled expression engraving deeper lines beside his mouth. 'But I must admit, I expected something different from Rachid, and his attitude definitely restores a little of my fait! in him. Abby, in his country, it must be extremely difficult to sustain continuity without a direct descendant. He's the eldest son, perhaps unfortunately, and it's his role to beget an heir.'

'Beget! Beget!' Abby gave a groan of exasperation. 'Honestly, Dad, you're beginning to sound like the book of Genesis! Rachid's brother has two sons already. Isn't that direct enough for you?'

Her father hesitated. 'If Rachid divorced you, there's every possibility that he could find a wife who would produce him a son,' he commented mildly, and Abby realised she had spoken as if she was still in the picture.

'As you say,' she agreed shortly, picking up a sandwich. 'And as far as I'm concerned, I wish he would do just that.'

Later that night, undressing in the quiet isolation of her room, Abby wondered what she would do if Rachid divorced her. It was all very well, talking blandly of getting married again, but somehow she knew that was most unlikely. Her experiences with Rachid had left her badly scarred, and where once there had been warmth and tenderness, now there was just a cold hard core of bitterness and resentment. She doubted any man could breach the defences she had built around herself, and she didn't really want anyone to try. It was better to be free, and independent, as she had told her father. Better not to love at all than to go though the pain and turmoil of those last months with Rachid. She was safe now, immune from the arrows of distrust and jealousy, secure within the shell of her own indifference. She had no desire to expose herself again, to lay open the paths to vulnerability and suffering. If she ever did allow another man into her life, she would make sure her involvement was not emotional. Emotions caused too many tortured days and sleepless nights.

Nevertheless, for the first time in months she found herself viewing her own body with something other than dissatisfaction. For so long she had regarded herself with discontented eyes, finding the lissom curves of her figure less than gratifying. She had seen no beauty in the swelling symmetry of her breasts, in the narrow waist and gently rounded thighs, that hinted of the sensual depths Rachid had once plumbed. All she had seen was a hollow vessel, lacking the essential constituents which would have made her a whole being. She was that most pathetic of all creatures, a barren woman, and all the allure and enticement of her body went for nothing beside such an elemental deficiency.

She twisted restlessly, turning sideways, looking at the pale oval of her face over her shoulder. On impulse, she reached up and released the coil of hair at her nape, and shards of silk fell almost to her waist. Her hair was one thing she would not change, straight and silky, and moonbeam-fair. Rachid had loved its soft fragrance, had liked nothing better than to bury his face in its lustrous curtain, and it was pure indulgence that she had not had it cut when she left Abarein. It was really too much for a working girl to handle, but it was her one extravagance, and she was loath to destroy it.

Now, spreading smoothly across her shoulders, concealing the thrusting peaks of womanhood, it accentuated her femininity, and she reflected sadly on the fates that had given her so much, yet denied her so much more.

Between the cotton sheets, she tried to dispel the unbidden fruits of memory. She didn't want to think about her life with Rachid. She had thought about that too much already. Too many nights, in those early days after their separation, she had cried herself to sleep for the cruel tragedy of it all, and now she preferred to forget that it had

not all been bad. On the contrary, in the beginning
she had almost too much happiness, and each
morning she had awakened eager to start the day.
She could not get too much of Rachid, nor he of
her, and she had resented those occasions when
business, or the affairs of state, had taken him
from her.

Unwillingly she recalled the first time she had
seen him—at that party in Paris, which had
proved such a fateful affair. She had gone to Paris
with Brad, to attend a conference called by the
oil-producing states, and the request to attend the
gathering at the Abareinian Embassy had been
just another invitation among many. Abby had
not even wanted to go, eager to sample the more
exciting night life to be found in Montmartre, but
Brad had been persuasive, and she had succumbed. After all, they were to be there for
several days more, and besides, he had promised
to take her sightseeing as soon as they could
decently make their escape.

In the event, it had not been Brad who showed
her Paris, but Rachid. The party at the Embassy
had not turned out at all as she had expected, and
looking back on it now, she could still feel the
thrill of excitement that had coursed through her
veins when he had first laid eyes on her. It was
the first time she had experienced such a tangible
reaction to an intangible contact, and she
remembered how put out Brad had been when
Rachid relieved him of his companion.

Parties at Middle Eastern embassies were usually sumptuous, with plenty of food and drink
provided for their European guests. Arabs, or at

least Muslims, did not touch alcohol, but they had no inhibitions about providing it for their visitors. They were extravagant affairs, with a great deal of business mixed in with the socialising, and even Abby, who was not unaccustomed to the attentions of the opposite sex tended to cling to Brad like a lifeline in a stormy sea.

Meeting Rachid was different however. He had been there, with his father, Prince Khalid, welcoming their guests when Abby and Brad arrived. Tall and dark, with strong, tanned features, and eyes so deep as to be almost black, he nevertheless possessed a less hawklike profile than his father, whose looks were distinctly those of an Arab. Rachid displayed his English ancestry, in the thick length of his lashes, in the lighter cast of his skin, and the sensually attractive curve of his mouth. He had a sense of humour, too, which was something she learned his father lacked, and his lean muscular frame complemented the well-cut dinner suit, that contrasted sharply with his father's robes and *kaffiyeh*.

Abby, at nineteen, had considered herself well capable of handling any situation. She had been Brad Daley's secretary for over a year, and during that time she had countered the advances of men from various backgrounds, and while she was attracted to Prince Rachid, she was immediately suspicious of his motives. Men of his wealth and education did not get seriously involved with secretaries, and while she enjoyed his attention, she tried not to respond to his undoubted sexual magnetism.

It proved difficult—and ultimately, impossible. Despite the quite obvious disapproval of his father and the rest of his family, Rachid neglected his other guests to remain at her side during the course of the evening, and afterwards, with Brad's grudging consent, he took her back to the hotel. He had been quite circumspect then, merely kissing her hand on departing, and wishing her a good night's sleep, and even when the sheaves of white roses began to arrive in the morning, she had had no conception of how hopeless would be her attempts to resist him.

He arrived at ten o'clock to take her sightseeing, and sweeping Brad's objections aside with the assurance that he would arrange for a temporary secretary to replace her, he took Abby on a tour of the city that left her speechless and breathless. He knew Paris intimately, having spent some time studying at the Sorbonne, and instead of whisking her from place to place in a limousine, he made her walk miles and miles through the fascinating heart of the city, until her feet ached, and she begged for relief.

Then he took her back to his hotel, instead of hers, much to her alarm, insisting that she must eat dinner with him, and that he did not intend to share her with Brad Daley. However, when she discovered that he intended ordering the meal served in his suite, she firmly declined, and only accompanied him upstairs to avoid standing alone in the lobby while he changed.

The hotel room had been magnificent, she remembered, with soft pile carpets and lots of concealed lighting. While Rachid disappeared into his bedroom, she kicked off her shoes and

curled on a soft couch, and would have fallen
asleep had not nervousness kept her awake.

He returned wearing not the casual pants and
matching jerkin he had worn all day, but a robe,
similar to the one his father had worn the night
before, only striped in shades of blue and purple
that accentuated the raven darkness of his hair.

Abby remembered she had been studying a
painting on the wall above a polished *escritoire*,
and her first intimation that she was no longer
alone had come when firm, strong fingers had
begun massaging her aching instep. She had been
shocked to find Rachid squatting at her feet, per-
forming the menial service, and had begun to
protest when he had lowered his head and
caressed her toes with his lips.

Her skin had burned through the fine mesh of
her tights, and when he had lifted his eyes to look
at her, her head had swum with the message she
read in their depths. For the first time in her life
she had encountered a man, and a situation, she
could not control, and her preconceived ideas of
the relationship between the sexes were violently
revised.

Her startled use of his name was a further dem-
onstration of how his actions disturbed her. All
day she had maintained the formality between
them, but suddenly they were no longer a Middle
Eastern prince and a secretary, but a man and a
woman caught in the oldest spell since creation.

Even so, she had clung to some semblance of
dignity, scrambling off the couch and putting the
width of the room between them. She couldn't
leave. Her shoes still lay near Rachid's straighten-

ing figure, and she could imagine the scandal which would ensue if she ran from the room in her stockinged feet. But she needed a breathing space, and the palpitating beat of her heart was evidence of the powerful effect he had on her.

Contrarily, Rachid had not pursued the issue. With a gesture of indifference he had left her, returning minutes later wearing a fine mohair lounge suit and the tie that proclaimed the exclusiveness of his public school, and much to Abby's bemusement, they had dined downstairs without another word being said about what had happened upstairs.

The following morning he arrived at her hotel before she was even dressed. Her room was still druggingly scented with the perfumes of the roses he had had delivered the previous day, and the chambermaid gushed admiringly as she brought an armful of pale pink orchids to join them.

'*Que Monsieur est romantique!*' she exclaimed, fingering the thick luscious petals, but Abby thought *single-minded* was probably a more apt description.

Nevertheless, she was aware her fingers had trembled so much she had dropped the soap in the shower, and she had deliberately dressed in her least feminine outfit to combat the emotions she was trying hard to suppress. She knew what he was doing. She had heard stories of other girls courted in this way. But somehow, imperatively, she must keep her head.

Unfortunately, despite what she later learned of Rachid's dislike of women in trousers, the wine silk shirt and toning velvet pants she had chosen merely accentuated the delicate swell of her woman's body, and with her hair straight to her waist and confined at her nape with a leather thong, she had looked both absurdly young and infinitely feminine. Rachid had not been able to take his eyes off her when she met him in the lobby of the hotel, and in spite of her earlier determination to refuse him, she found herself accepting his invitation to drive with him to Versailles.

He drove himself, an infrequent occurrence, she later learned, but in this instance essential to their privacy. They had wandered together through the magnificent park and gardens of the palace, gazing at the flowerbeds and ornamental lakes, the statuary and the fountains, and when Rachid captured her hand to draw her attention to the spectacular chariot rising from the waters of the Bassin d'Apollon, it seemed natural that her fingers should remain within the firm coolness of his.

It was another wonderful day, and by the time they drove back to Paris, Abby had almost forgotten the reasons which had brought her there in the first place. Unfortunately Brad had not, and the row that ensued on her return made her realise how selfishly she was behaving. His diatribe, too, on the recklessness of what she was doing did not improve the situation, particularly as he was only saying the things she herself had thought previously, and which even now were struggling for existence. He said she was a fool, and an innocent if she imagined the Prince Rachid Hasan al Juhami wanted anything more than to satisfy his lust for her body, and that if that didn't trouble her the way Arabs treated their women would. They were just chattels, he maintained, there to satisfy a purpose, but without any rights to take enjoyment from it.

Abby had been shocked and appalled by the things he had said. Brad was not a prude, and he had no way of knowing whether or not she was still a virgin, and she half believed his outraged indignation. The fact that she had never been with a man made his words that much more terrifying, and while her senses rejected his angry denigration, her frightened logic could not.

In consequence, when Rachid arrived the following morning she refused to see him, and spent the day with Brad, attending a business meeting in the morning and lecture in the afternoon. She had told herself it was the sensible thing to do, and even though that night had been the first of the many when she cried herself to sleep over Rachid, she was convinced it was the only thing to do.

Unfortunately, the following day brought her into contact with the Abareinian delegation once more. Attending a reception at one of the other embassies, Rachid was the first man she saw on their arrival, and in spite of her determination, her eyes were drawn again and again to his dark-suited figure. Not that Rachid appeared to notice. He seemed quite content to remain with his own party, listening to what his colleagues had to say in that distinctive way he had of inclining his dark head in their direction, a faint smile of acknowledgement tugging at the corners of his mobile mouth.

Naturally Brad had been well pleased that his advice had appeared to work, and if he noticed that Abby's lips were a little tighter when they left the Embassy, and her smile a little forced, he feigned ignorance. With supreme indifference to the fact that she had already been there with Rachid, he took her to the Louvre, and they spent the rest of the afternoon walking through the museums that house the most important artistic collection in the world, before returning to their hotel to take dinner in the restaurant.

By the time she left Brad in the foyer of the hotel, Abby's head was aching and there was a curiously hollow feeling inside her, despite the excellence of the food she had just consumed. She put it down to fatigue and nervous exhaustion, but as she rode up in the lift she knew it was due in no small part to Rachid's defection. It was to be expected, of course, after the way she had behaved, but she was amazed at the turmoil it had left inside her.

Her room was on the tenth floor, overlooking the Place de la Concorde, but this evening she had no interest in her surroundings. She felt raw and vulnerable, and it was not a pleasant experience. To alleviate her discomfort, she decided to take a bath, and minutes later, relaxing in the soapy scented water, she felt she had made the right decision. The water was warm and soothing, and swirled about her like a protective cocoon.

The knock that was repeated at the outer door dispelled the brief illusion of immunity. Guessing it was Brad with some instructions for the morning, she called to him to wait, and quickly patted herself dry before donning the ankle-length towelling robe which she normally used as a dressing gown. With her hair spilling from an improvised knot on top of her head, and the robe wrapped securely about her, she opened the door, and then expelled her breath on a gasp when she found Rachid on the threshold.

'Can I come in?' he asked, and she was convinced that no single item of her state of *déshabille* had escaped his notice. The dark eyes were all-encompassing, and she clutched the lapels of the towelling robe as if it was essential to hide every inch of burning flesh from him.

'It's late,' she said foolishly, realising a more vehement refusal should have been forthcoming, but his unexpected appearance when she was feeling most susceptible had temporarily robbed her of calm reasoning.

'I have to talk to you,' he insisted, supporting himself with one hand against the door frame, the lapels of his jacket falling open to reveal the shadowy outline of his chest beneath the sheer silk of his shirt. 'Abby, I beg of you, let me come in. At least for a moment. I would prefer not to be seen hanging about your bedroom door at this time of night, if possible.'

His words hardened her resolve. 'Then go,' she said tightly. 'No one asked you to come here.'

'Abby!'

The night-dark irises pleaded with her, and combined with the magnetic appeal of the man himself, they were a potent seducement. Moving her head silently from side to side, not trusting herself to speak, she tried to close the door, but his foot was in the way and with a little sound of protest she fell back from him, seeking the farthest corner of the room. He must not know how he affected her, she thought desperately, but how could she disguise it?

Rachid came into the room slowly, closing the door behind him and leaning his broad shoulders back against the panels. Then, tipping his head on one side, he looked at her with half reproachful impatience.

'Why are you frightened of me?' he asked, dark brows drawing together above the faintly arrogant curve of his nose. 'What did I do to make you afraid of me? And why did you refuse to see me yesterday? Do we not enjoy ourselves together? I was under the impression that you liked my company. Was I wrong?'

Abby didn't know how to answer him. To tell him that she had not enjoyed their time together would be an outright lie, yet to admit the contrary would be to invite who knew what familiarities.

'I—did find your company—informative,' she ventured at last, choosing her words carefully. 'You obviously know Paris very well, and your knowledge of Versailles—'

'I did not mean that, and you know it,' he exclaimed, pushing himself away from the door and moving towards her with a firm pantherlike tread. 'We were beginning to know one another, that is the important thing, and I want to know why you chose to sever our relationship with the sensitivity of a camel driver!'

He came round the end of her bed, imprisoning her in a corner of the room with no escape except across the bed itself. Abby considered climbing across the counter-pane, but such behaviour seemed undignified, and besides, if he attacked her she could always scream. Brad's room was next door, and by now he must surely have finished the drink he had intended to have in the bar before coming upstairs.

'I think you ought to go, Prince Rachid,' she insisted tremulously, endeavouring not to look as anxious as she felt. 'It—it was good of you to give me your time, but—'

'It was not good at all,' he interrupted roughly, now only inches away from her. 'I wanted to spend my time with you, Abby. I can think of nothing I have enjoyed more, and—' he reached out a hand to touch her cheek, '—I do not believe you did not enjoy it, too.'

Abby's instinctive flinching away from him brought a faint flush of anger to his cheeks. '*Haji*, what is wrong with you?' he demanded, gazing down at her without comprehension. 'What kind of man do you think I am that you tremble like a gazelle just because I lay my hand on you?'

'Please go,' she got out chokingly, panic rising unbidden inside her. 'Please, I want you to leave. At—at once. And I never want to see you again.'

'No? Is this so? And what has happened to change your mind?'

He was so close now that she could see the flecks of lightness in those dark eyes, approve the texture of his skin, that was firm and tanned, and only slightly shadowed by the shaven growth

of his beard. She could see the strong column of
his throat rising from the collar of his shirt, and
smell the clean odour of his body, mingling with
that of his clothes and his shaving lotion. His hair
clung smoothly to the shape of his head, free of
any of the greasy dressings some men needed to
keep their hair in order, and beneath the flaring
pendulum of his tie his quickened breathing
strained the buttons of his shirt. Her eyes dropped
lower, only to dart up again swiftly, in case he
imagined she was as curious about him as he
appeared to be about her.

'Prince Rachid—'

'Rachid will do.'

'Rachid, then. . .'

She put out a hand to ward him off, but he was
too close. Her fingers made contact with the taut
silk that covered his chest, and as they recoiled
in embarrassment he bent his head and touched
her ear with his lips.

It was the lightest caress, a brief meeting of
the flesh, but Abby quivered in the grip of emotions far greater than the touch warranted, and as
if compelled in spite of himself, he slipped an arm
around her waist and brought her close against his
hard body.

'Rachid—' she began again, more frantically
now, but the smouldering passion of his gaze
rendered her speechless. Almost involuntarily her
lips parted, and this time when he bent his head,
his mouth found hers.

It was a devastating experience, the firmness
of his lips tasting hers with sensuous enjoyment.
She felt a dizzying sense of imbalance in the

increasing pressure of his embrace, and her hands groped blindly for his lapels in an effort to maintain some hold on reality. She was imprisoned against him, her breasts crushed by the sinewy strength of his chest, the bones of her hips melting against the powerful muscles of his thighs.

'Abby. . .'

He said her name against her mouth, and a weak sense of inadequacy gripped her. She was no match for his experienced advances, and contrary to what Brad had told her, Rachid was no amateur in the matter of sensitivity. His whole approach was skilful, measured, and she was helpless against the sensual needs he was deliberately arousing. There was no need for brutality, no need to force her at all. In his hands, with the pulsating heat of his desire thrusting against her, she only wanted to respond, and her moan of submission was as much a plea for possession as a protest at his undoubted expertise.

With unhurried movements he slid the towelling robe from her shoulders, his mouth tracing its passing with lingering pleasure. Then, when she was desperately trying to recover her modesty, his hands loosened the cord that circled her waist so that the robe fell open before him.

'Rachid, *no*. . .' she gasped, but her denial was submerged beneath the sharp thrill of indulgence she felt when his long fingers cupped the swollen fullness of her breast.

'Beautiful,' he said, his voice low and husky with emotion. 'So perfectly formed. So round and pink and delicious. I must taste. . .'

'Oh, Rachid,' she whispered tremulously, as

his tongue probed the roseate peak, and his eyes narrowed with emotive anticipation.

'You do not really want me to stop, do you?' he murmured, as the towelling robe fell to the floor. 'Do not be ashamed of your body. It is a temple at which I worship, and never have I held so much beauty in my hands.'

Abby was totally bemused. She had never shared such intimacy with any man, but when he tossed off his own jacket and tie, and unfastened the buttons of his shirt, the lingering memory of Brad's insinuations returned to torment her.

'I—I can't,' she got out chokingly, as he swung her up into his arms and lifted her on to the bed. 'Rachid, I haven't—I've never—'

'Do you think I do not know that?' he demanded huskily, lowering his weight beside her. 'But do not be afraid. I will not hurt you. I will just caress you—so, and you will have nothing to fear.'

Abby's trembling limbs were weak with longings she hardly knew or understood, but still she had to understand him. 'You mean—you mean—you're not going to—to—'

'—make love to you?' he finished, nuzzling her shoulder with his lips. 'Not if you do not want to, no. There are—other ways of pleasing one another, and if you are afraid. . .'

'Oh, Rachid. . .'

Relief made her wind her arms around his neck, bringing his mouth down to hers with hungry urgency, and the burning pressure of his mouth ignited the stirring flame inside her. Hardly aware of what she was doing, she moved beneath him

eagerly, arching against his hard length, until only
the layer of his clothes separated her from his
throbbing possession.

'Abby. . .'

Now it was Rachid who protested her inno-
cence, but the imprisoning weight of his body
drove all desire to resist from her, and her mouth
opened beneath his.

The smooth expanse of his chest spread
beneath her palms, warm and male, and only
slightly roughened by the fine dark hair that was
abrasively virile to the touch. Her hands investi-
gated his shoulders, her nails probing the hollows
of his ears, the strong column of his neck where
the hair grew down to his nape. She wanted to
know every inch of him, and time and place were
forgotten in the delights of exploration.

Rachid's mouth devoured hers as his hands
searched the curve of her waist and the swell of
her hips. His touch aroused her to unknown
heights of excitement and anticipation, and she
was all yielding woman in his arms.

She heard his muffled imprecation when her
fingers found the buckle of his belt, but by then
neither of them was capable of thinking beyond
the moment, and the moment demanded surrender. With a groan of submission, Rachid lost what
little control he had left, and his legs parted hers.

The heat of him against her promoted its own
consummation. What happened was as natural as
the turning of the season, and Abby's cry of pain
was stifled beneath the probing hunger of his kiss.
She was hardly aware of the moment when he
started to move within her, or indeed of the

moment when the pressure began to build. But it happened, and they climbed together, scaling the boundaries of human experience, reaching the peak of sensual fulfilment. It was an unbelievable sensation, and looking up into Rachid's sweat-moistened features, Abby knew that he was feeling it too. They sank together through the veils of shimmering ecstasy, and it was she who sought his lips with hers in the glorious aftermath of their lovemaking.

CHAPTER THREE

ABBY'S body was moist now, as she moved restlessly beneath the bedcovers, striving to dispel those images that threatened to destroy her newfound peace of mind. Rachid was good in bed, they were good together, she told herself, with enforced detachment, but that did not mean he was not equally good with someone else.

A pain twisted in her stomach, and to disperse it she allowed the images to return. She remembered how appalled she had been when the drugging mists of their lovemaking had cleared, and she had to acknowledge to herself what she had done, what Rachid had done. She had wanted to escape him there and then, but his hands had secured her beside him, and in a calm but decisive voice, he had told her he intended to marry her.

She had been at first incredulous, then hysterically amused, and finally tearfully reproachful. She told him he should not joke about so serious a matter, and in consequence he had become quite angry. He was perfectly serious, he insisted. He had thought of little else but her since he first laid eyes upon her, and this evening he had waited in proven impatience to tell her so.

Abby recalled how doubtful she had been, how anxious to believe him, and yet so unwilling to accept that he actually loved her. She had brought up his avoidance of her at the previous day's

reception, and how she had cried herself to sleep
the night before, and far from feeling ashamed
of himself, Rachid had been quite delighted. He
had attended the reception deliberately in the
hope that he might see her, he said, and her reactions had been exactly what he had hoped for.
Unfortunately, he had not been able to avoid his
own responsibilities the following morning, and
by the time he arrived at the hotel Abby had
already left on the sightseeing outing Brad had
arranged.

Rachid's words had both exasperated and flat-
tered her. His sincerity was no longer in any
doubt, and gradually she had started to believe
him. He meant what he said, he insisted. She was
all he had ever wanted in a woman, and by the
following morning she was totally convinced.

Brad's reactions had been predictably aggressive. When he learned what had happened, he had
been absolutely appalled, and far from wishing
her well, he had told her she was a fool if she
believed Rachid's father would countenance such
a marriage. He had almost persuaded her that she
had imagined Rachid's proposal, so that when
she saw him again she had been cool and aloof,
and nervously sceptical of his ardour.

Looking back on it now, Abby realised how
tenacious Rachid had been in his pursuit of her.
Whether there had been a certain amount of jealous determination mixed in with his professed
love for her, she could not be completely sure,
but whatever his motivation, she had not been
allowed to ignore him. And besides, she hadn't
wanted to. She had loved him, that was never

in question, and it was only later that she had discovered his ideas of love and hers were vastly different.

Even so, in those early days, he had been all she had ever dreamed of in a lover, and the weeks and months after their wedding had been the happiest of her life. Even his father had not been able to hurt her then, and Prince Khalid's initial opposition to the marriage had melted beneath his obvious delight in his eldest son's contentment. Abby's own parents had had misgivings, too, but they trusted her and wanted her happiness above all things, and in the first flush of her relationship with Rachid, Abby had been idyllically so.

With a groan, Abby buried her face in the pillow now, trying to expunge the agonies that memory could bring. She had gone far enough in her recollecting. She didn't want to remember what came after. She didn't want to think of pain and humiliation, and ultimately disillusionment. That was all over now, and she was determined it would remain so.

The next morning she was pale and heavy-eyed when she entered her office and she was glad Brad was late in arriving. It gave her time to get busy at her desk, so that when he appeared she could greet him with an absent smile, as if absorbed with the quota schedules she was typing.

Brad, however, was more astute than she thought, and his thoughtful appraisal deepened to a concerned regard when she barely lifted her face to his.

'You look tired,' he said, stopping in front of her desk and tapping its surface with his fingers.

He was not a tall man, but he was stockily built, and his sturdy figure had a blunt persistence. 'What time did you get home from Liz's last night? I've told you before about burning the candle at both ends. You should listen to me.'

Abby summoned a faint smile. 'Honestly, Brad, you sound more like a mother than an employer! All right, so I'm tired. I didn't sleep very well, as it happens. Does that satisfy you?'

'You didn't answer my question,' retorted Brad dogmatically. 'I asked what time you got home from Liz Forster's. I know she was giving a party—you told me so yourself.'

'Did I?' Abby was finding it incredibly difficult to remember anything that happened the previous day before that fateful encounter with Rachid. 'Oh, yes, so I did. Well, yes, I went—but I got home quite early. A-about ten o'clock, I think.'

Brad studied her determinedly downbent head with veiled impatience. 'And did you enjoy it?'

'Enjoy it? Enjoy what?' Abby looked up almost blankly.

'The party!' Brad replied forcefully. 'Liz's party! I asked if you—'

'—enjoyed it. Yes, of course.' Abby chewed on her lower lip. 'Yes, it was all right. You know what Liz's parties are like. Lots of food and wine and music. Good company—'

Brad shook his head. 'So why did you leave early?'

'Is this an inquisition?' Abby jerked the sheets of paper out of the typewriter. 'Damn these things! I always have to do them twice.'

Brad hesitated a moment longer, and then as Abby got up from her desk to marshall another batch of carbons, he shrugged and walked through the door into his own office. He was not appeased, Abby guessed, but short of demanding a résumé of her evening's activities, he knew he was unlikely to get a satisfactory answer.

The rest of his morning was taken up with meetings, and by the time he got around to dictating his letters that afternoon, he had other things on his mind. Besides, by then, Abby had applied a light blusher to her cheeks and erased the circles around her eyes with careful make-up, and her appearance evidently allayed any lingering suspicions he had. Since she had returned to work for him, he had adopted a kind of proprietorial interest in her affairs, and while she appreciated his protection, there were times, as now, when she felt the restraints it put upon her. She knew he had her well-being at heart. He obviously blamed himself in some part for her disastrous relationship with Rachid. But he was a bachelor, after all, despite the fact that he was in his forties, and she knew the girls in the office saw his interest in an entirely different light. She sometimes wondered if he was attracted to her in that way, particularly if he showed his impatience when one or other of the male members of his staff displayed any interest in her, and maybe her own abnegation of their overtures was partly to blame. But she had never confided the whole truth of her separation from Rachid to anyone, and although the facts were blatant enough, no one knew how emotionally enfeebling the break-up had been. She doubted her ability to enjoy a fulfilling relationship with any man ever again, and she was tempted to tell Brad he was guarding an empty shell.

It was dark when she left the office that evening, even though it was only a little after five-thirty. Winter was drawing in, and already there was an icy chill in the air. The lamps of Marlborough Mews cast a mellow glow, however, and beyond, the busier thoroughfares were a mass of changing lights. Abby could hear the roar of the traffic and the impatient honking of car horns, and she couldn't help a momentary pang of nostalgia. In Abarein at this time of the year, the weather would be just cooling after the powerful heat of summer. During the day it would be a pleasant seventy-five or eighty degrees, with blue skies all day long and velvety nights to look forward to. It was the time of year when it was possible to sit in the sun or swim in the pool, or laze in the coolness of a shadowy courtyard, redolent with the heady perfumes of flowering vines and fig trees.

Shaking away the feelings of melancholy her thoughts had evoked, Abby hurried along the street towards the underground station. It was pointless indulging in sentimentality, particularly when sentiment had played so small a part in her life there, and she felt impatient with herself for allowing the past to haunt her. But it had been seeing Rachid again which had triggered all these remembrances, and she guessed it had been his intention to arouse just such a reaction.

Riding home in the train, she turned her atten-

tion to more immediate matters. The question of
what she and her father were to have for their
evening meal was her most pressing problem, and
she spent the remainder of the journey turning
the contents of the refrigerator over in her mind.
There were always eggs, she thought wryly, considering omelettes, but somehow food had lost the
ability to evoke any enthusiasm at the moment.

Dacre Mews seemed dimly lit as she turned off
Dartford Road. The tall, narrow houses clustered
together, shutting out the stars, and etching themselves darkly against the night sky. There were
lights in some of the windows, but it was early
as yet, and many of the tenants had not returned
home from their jobs in the city. It was a working
community, and Professor Gillespie enjoyed his
isolation during the day.

The Mews was gradually filling with cars, and
Abby picked her way between them, glad that
she did not have to find somewhere to park. Her
father's old Alvis spent most of its days in the
garage, and since leaving Rachid she had not
found the use for a car. She knew it annoyed her
father that in the evenings there was invariably a
car parked at their gate, but fortunately his days
were left undisturbed.

There was a car parked outside their house this
evening, she saw, as she crossed the strip of grass
that some enthusiastic gardener had planted
between the flagstones. A big car, long and black
and expensive—

She halted abruptly. She knew that car. It was
the same car that had brought her home the previous evening. It was the Mercedes. Rachid's car!

Briefly, panic gripped her. What was he doing here, at her house, talking with her father? Why had he come? Why couldn't he leave her alone? She didn't want to see him; she didn't want to talk to him. They had nothing to say to one another. Why wouldn't he accept that?

She stood there, struggling to contain her emotions, her breathing shallow as her pulses quickened. She knew an almost irresistible urge to turn and run out of the Mews, and keep running until she discovered some place where Rachid would never find her. She didn't want to face him. She didn't want to fight him. She just wanted to be left alone.

But as she stood there, and people passed her, looking at her with curious eyes, she knew she could not run away. It would achieve nothing. Sooner or later Rachid would find her again, and then the whole process would have to be repeated. Besides, if she ran away, it would appear that she was *afraid* to face him, that she had something to hide—her feelings maybe!

She expelled her breath on a long sigh, endeavouring to regain her composure. This was ridiculous, she told herself severely. She was behaving like a schoolgirl. First, last evening, now today. She had to get a hold of herself, and stop behaving as if Rachid had some extraordinary power over her. He couldn't *make* her go back with him, he wouldn't *force* her. And surely, after all she had gone through, she had the determination not to let him intimidate her in this way. Remember Farah, she reminded herself harshly, and unconsciously her shoulders stiffened.

Taking a deep breath, she walked the last few yards to the shallow steps that led up to the front door. As she fumbled for her key, she gave the car another swift appraisal. Yes, it was definitely Rachid's car, she confirmed tightly, with the man Ahmed, inclining his head politely to her from his position behind the wheel.

Pressing her lips together, she inserted her key in the lock and opened the door. No matter how nervous she might inwardly be, she had to appear calm and controlled, but her fingers trembled as she dropped the latch behind her.

Her father appeared in the doorway of his study as she was removing her coat. He looked anxious, too, she thought and she wondered if he thought she might blame him for Rachid's presence. Forcing a tense smile, she tried to convey that she understood his dilemma, and his features relaxed as he indicated the room behind him.

'Rachid's here,' he said unnecessarily. 'We've been waiting for you. Have you had a good day?'

His words were so trite and ordinary, he might have been speaking about the weather, but Abby decided it was probably the best way to behave. If they acted as though Rachid's arrival could in any way disrupt their lives, they were courting disaster, and the only thing to do was to treat him with the offhand courtesy of a casual visitor.

'It's been—a busy day,' she said now, casting a fleeting look at her reflection in the mirror above the umbrella stand. She looked flushed, she thought, wishing that she didn't, but at least her hair was neat, and the dark skirt and matching waistcoat were formal and businesslike. 'How are you? Did you go to the library?'

'Actually, no,' answered her father quietly, his eyes darting meaningfully towards the room behind him. 'I didn't have time. Rachid arrived about three o'clock.'

Abby nodded, and realising she could not put it off any longer, she allowed her father to step back and let her precede him into his study.

Rachid had obviously risen when her father left the room, and now he was standing with his back to a glass-fronted bookcase. In the lamp-light, he looked dark and faintly menacing, although his expression was enigmatic as Abby came into his view. He was wearing a dark suit this evening, a soft sienna-brown suede, the jacket parting over a bronze silk shirt, the trousers moulding the powerful muscles of his thighs. Long legs were spread, his hands locked behind his back, the smooth virility of his hair glinting with raven lights.

'Abby,' he murmured politely, as she entered the room, making no move to touch her or offer a greeting, and she glanced behind her as her father joined them, wondering exactly what conversation had taken place in her absence.

'Sherry?' suggested Professor Gillespie briskly, crossing to a tray set on a table in the corner. 'Abby? You'll have a glass, won't you? How about you, Rachid? Will you taste the vine?'

Rachid shook his head, and Abby subsided on to the low couch her father used when he wanted to relax. Had he been absorbed into the dictates of his father's religion at last? she wondered, feeling a slight chill of apprehension along her spine.

It was all very well telling Liz that Rachid was a Muslim, when she really believed he was not, and quite another to run up against the implacable force of will that abhorred the use of alcohol and upheld the rights of man. She accepted the glass of sherry her father handed her with some relief, and took refuge in its warming contents that moistened the dryness of her mouth.

'Can I get you a beer, or some tonic water?' Professor Gillespie persisted, looking at Rachid again, but his guest merely shook his head once more.

'Nothing, thank you,' he affirmed with civility, and Abby's father made an apologetic gesture as he raised his own glass to his lips.

Abby waited for Rachid to speak, but again it was her father who made the first overture. 'Would you like me to leave you alone?' he suggested, unwilling to intrude, but Abby forestalled his departure with a heated denial.

'I think Rachid should tell me why he's come here,' she declared, permitting herself a brief glance up at her husband. It was all very well telling herself that she had to remain calm, but beneath Rachid's faintly supercilious regard, she was growing resentful. 'I can't imagine what he feels he has to say to me, particularly after our conversation last night, and if anyone has to leave, I think it should be him!'

There was silence for a few moments after her statement, and she was aware of her father's discomfort at being a party to their conflict. But there was no other way to deal with Rachid, and her own nerves were ragged by the time he chose to answer her.

'I should be very grateful if you would leave us alone for a few minutes, Professor,' said Rachid, with quiet decisiveness, ignoring Abby's gasping indignation. 'You know why I am here. Surely it is not so much to ask—a few minutes alone with my wife?'

'I'm not your wife—' Abby was beginning, but her father was moving towards the door.

'I'll be upstairs,' he said, giving her a vaguely persuasive look, and she knew that so far as he was concerned she ought to give Rachid the benefit of a hearing.

The door closed behind him, and Abby stilled the instinct to get to her feet. She was safer sitting down, she decided. She did not entirely trust her legs to support her, and besides, she could avoid his gaze more easily this way.

Rachid, however, had other ideas. Just when she had convinced herself she was in control of the situation, he crossed the square of carpet and lowered himself on to the couch beside her, his superior weight causing the cushions to compress, creating a sloping incline she had to combat.

'So, Abby,' he murmured, turning sideways to look at her, 'you are afraid of me!'

'Me? Afraid of you?' Abby managed a gasp of contempt. 'Don't be so ridiculous!'

Rachid shrugged. 'Why else do you behave like a startled dove, just because I wish speech with you?'

Abby sighed. 'We have nothing to say to one another, Rachid. I told you last night—'

'Last night you were shocked. You had not expected to see me at the party. I realise now, that was a mistake. I should not have appeared in front of you like that. I should have telephoned you first, written to you—'

'Rachid, it wouldn't have made the slightest difference.' Abby took a deep breath. 'Why won't you understand? It's over. Our life together is over!'

'No!' His features hardened perceptibly, a muscle beating erratically at his jawline. 'I will never accept that, Abby. You are my wife, my—my—'

'Possession?' she supplied coldly, turning to look at him. 'That is how you see me, isn't it? Your woman? Your chattel—'

'For the love of God, be still,' he muttered, anger darkening his lean features. 'Why do you persist in fighting me? Why can you not accept what I am offering you?'

'Because it's not enough,' she retorted, rising now, unable to still her trembling limbs any longer. 'Why won't you accept that I don't love you any more, Rachid? Why can't you see that you're wasting your time?'

'Your father does not think so,' he intoned harshly, getting to his feet behind her so that she swung round nervously, alert to his every move. 'He is of the opinion that you are distrait, uncertain, unable to make such a decision for yourself.'

'My father said that!' Abby was horrified.

'Not in so many words.' Rachid's quiet admission restored a little of her faith. 'But he agrees with me that you should think most seriously before making up your mind.'

'Making up my mind?' echoed Abby blankly. 'Rachid, my mind *is* made up. I'm not coming back to you, and that's that.'

His hands clenched at his sides, and for a second she thought he was going to take hold of her and shake her into submission. It was a disturbing moment, a moment when her dark-lashed eyes gazed with tremulous challenge into his, and encountered the smouldering evidence of his anger. She was intimidated, but she knew if she faltered he would overwhelm her protests, and she forced herself to appear composed even though she was shaking inside.

'Is this your final word?' he enquired grimly, and silently she nodded.

'Very well.'

With a defeated gesture he turned aside, and her enforced stand crumbled. He was accepting her word, she thought disbelievingly, and the fruits of victory were like ashes in her mouth.

Rachid moved towards the door, but before opening it, he had something else to say. 'There is one thing I would ask of you,' he said quietly, his expression unreadable as she swung round on her heels, trying to appear unconcerned.

'Yes? What is it?'

'I wish you would have dinner with me tomorrow evening,' he said, much to her astonishment. 'There are matters we must discuss if you are determined to destroy our marriage, and I prefer to do my bargaining on my own ground, if you do not mind.'

Abby licked her dry lips. 'Your own ground. . .'

'My hotel,' he averred smoothly. 'You know it. Will you have dinner with me there at—say, eight o'clock tomorrow evening?'

Abby was cautious. 'How do I know—'

'Do you not think it is a small favour to ask?' he enquired, a little of the harshness returning to his tones at her hesitation. 'You are still my wife, Abby, whether you like it or not, and you owe me something for the time we spent together.'

Abby was tempted to argue, but there was a certain truth in what he said. She had had everything he could materially offer her, and perhaps she owed him something for that, if nothing else. Either way, she knew her father would not condone her denying him an evening of her company, and he was right, there were matters to discuss, not least their divorce.

'All right,' she said now, 'I'll come. But—'

'No buts, Abby,' he countered abruptly, cutting off her tentative qualification. 'Eight o'clock. I will expect you!' And pulling open the door, he wished her a curt good evening.

Her father appeared as soon as the outer door had closed behind Rachid, coming into the study enquiringly, his narrow face creased into a frown. He gave his daughter a curious glance, then said half apologetically:

'What could I do? He insisted on staying until you got back.'

Abby gave a sigh of resignation, and then put out her hand, as if in acknowledgement. 'I know. I know what Rachid's like. But what did you say to him? Did you let him think there was some chance that I might change my mind?'

'No!' But Professor Gillespie looked slightly discomfited by her candour. 'But—well, Abby, you know how I feel. Marriage is a sacred covenant, not to be entered into lightly. Nor should it be broken in the same way.'

Abby gasped. 'You think what Rachid did isn't a serious matter?'

Professor Gillespie fumbled for his pipe. 'I think you're too emotional, Abby. I always have. There's more to a relationship than—than the physical aspect. Your mother and I—'

'Were you ever unfaithful to Mummy?' demanded Abby hotly, overriding his protest. 'How many mistresses did you keep in various parts of the city?'

'Don't be ridiculous, child!' Her father's nostrils flared as he strove to keep his temper. 'You know perfectly well—'

'Yes, I know perfectly well that you never had any mistresses, nor did you sire any bastard children! And that's my point precisely. You can't compare your marriage to mine, or your behaviour with Rachid's!'

The following evening Abby dressed for her dinner date with increasing apprehension. All day she had fretted with uncertainty, tempted every other minute to ring the hotel and make some excuse. But she knew if she did, Rachid would only find some other way to see her, and at least this way she was prepared.

Nevertheless, she couldn't help wishing she

had held out for a more formal meeting, an interview in the company of his solicitor or hers, with all the protection that the legal profession could provide. She had been a fool to agree to this inevitably unpleasant tête-à-tête, but his unexpected capitulation had temporarily robbed her of her powers of reasoning. It had not helped to find her father had some sympathy with his cause, and since it was she, and not Rachid, who wanted to dissolve this marriage, Professor Gillespie was loath to give her his support.

She decided to wear trousers, as a deliberate assault on his ideas of femininity, the masculine attire strengthening her determination to show her independence. Black velvet pants accentuated the length of her legs, and the matching jerkin she wore with them concealed the revealing curves of her body. The long silky hair was coiled into a knot on the top of her head, and a velvet cap with a swinging tassel completed the image of staunch emancipation. Only as she walked was her sex unmistakable, the provocative swing of her hips proclaiming her womanhood.

But Abby, examining her reflection before she departed, was unaware of this betraying trait, and she was well pleased with the picture she represented. It was sombre, she thought, but that was how it should be, and if her stomach muscles tightened at the thought of how appropriate her appearance was in the circumstances, she determinedly thrust the feeling aside. At least Rachid should be in no doubt that she meant what she said, she decided with satisfaction, and throwing her sheepskin jacket about her shoulders, she went downstairs.

Fortunately, her father had a dinner engagement himself that evening, and as he had departed before her, she was not obliged to explain her destination. She felt a little deceitful, keeping it to herself, but she knew if she told him the truth it would only arouse hopes she could not possibly fulfil. So far as her father was concerned she and Rachid were finished, and tomorrow she would explain, after her husband had left for Abarein.

She took a taxi to the hotel and entered the lobby, not without a certain amount of trepidation. It was impossible not to feel apprehensive where Rachid was concerned, and besides, her surroundings alone were intimidating enough. He always stayed at the most exclusive hotel in London, and she was glad the velvet suit had been bought in New York and would therefore pass muster among so many glitteringly gowned and jewelled escorts. For herself, she wore little jewellery, only a thin gold chain around her neck, and the slim gold watch Rachid had bought her at Cartiers. The extravagant necklaces and bracelets he had bought had been left behind when she returned to England, and as she had never worn a lot of jewellery, she didn't miss them. All the same, her head turned as diamonds and sapphires and emeralds sparkled on ears and wrists, and she felt like the slender boy she resembled, wide-eyed in the cave of Aladdin.

There was no sign of Rachid, however, and as it was already after eight o'clock she approached the reception desk. Perhaps he had been unavoid-

ably detained, she thought hopefully, or maybe
he had had to return to Abarein at short notice.
Still, she knew in those circumstances he would
have contacted her, and her nerves were stretched
tautly as she crossed the cushioned pile of the
carpet.

The receptionist was female, and more inclined
to be generous to members of the opposite sex.
One look at Abby's pale, luminous face was
enough to convince her that this was no effemi-
nate boy but a slim and beautiful woman, and her
lips tightened perceptibly as she asked if she
could be of assistance.

'I have an appointment,' said Abby uncomfortably. 'With—er—with Prince Rachid. He is
staying at this hotel, isn't he?'

The girl frowned. 'You are—' she consulted a
pad in front of her, '—Princess Hiriz?'

Abby felt herself colouring. She wanted to say,
no, her name was Abigail Gillespie, but that
would have been a deliberate distortion of the
truth. Besides, the receptionist's expression was
such that she almost enjoyed acknowledging her
identity, even if it did evoke certain raised
eyebrows.

'You are?' The girl was clearly taken aback,
but she recovered herself quickly and went on:
'I'll get someone to escort you to Prince Rachid's
suite.' She prodded the bell on her desk. 'Suite
1101 please!'

'No—wait! That is—' Abby glanced about her
in embarrassment now. 'I was supposed to
meet—to meet Prince Rachid here, in the lobby.'

The receptionist's supercilious gaze returned

to her anxious face. 'You're sure you are Princess Hiriz?'

'Of course.' Abby was impatient now.

'Then surely you know that Prince Rachid was taken ill yesterday evening, and hasn't left his suite since?'

CHAPTER FOUR

ABBY's heated cheeks lost a little of their hectic colour. 'No,' she said definitely, shaking her head. 'No, I didn't know. I—er—I saw Prince Rachid yesterday evening and he seemed all right then.'

The receptionist shrugged. 'He left word that you were to be shown up to his suite upon your arrival. Do you wish me to arrange this or not?'

Abby shifted uncomfortably. 'You're sure he is ill?' she ventured, and then cringed at the look the other girl gave her. She was vaguely aware that one of the porters had come to stand beside her, no doubt acting upon the receptionist's instructions, and with a gesture of defeat, she gave in. 'Thank you,' she murmured, essaying her permission, and with a polite inclination of his head the man indicated the lifts.

They wafted up to the eleventh floor, the smoothness of their ascent cushioned by air pressure. There was a lingering aroma of perfume in the lift, evidence of its previous occupants, and the floors they passed in swift succession were discreetly-lit windows through the meshed glass doors.

All too soon, it seemed, they had reached their destination, and Abby stepped out on slightly unsteady legs on to the softly-woven carpet of the corridor. The porter led the way, and they traversed its honey-gold surface until they reached double-panelled white doors, edged in gilt. The numbers 1101 were secured in gold also, and at the porter's summons the doors were opened.

It was the man Karim, resplendent in his white robes and matching *kaffiyeh*. He bowed politely in Abby's direction, pressed a note of some denomination into the porter's hand, and then ushered his guest into the sitting room behind him.

It was a spacious apartment, carpeted in green, with yellow and cream striped sofas and chairs, and little polished tables holding vases of flowers. The room was redolent with their scent, a heady mixture to someone whose senses were already reeling from this unexpected turn of events.

'Princess!' Karim bowed again, and realising this might be her only opportunity to question him, Abby hurried into speech.

'The Prince,' she said, 'your master—is he really ill?'

'Did you doubt it?'

The voice came from behind her, and for a moment she was totally disorientated. Then, identifying those dark, liquid tones, she spun round to find Rachid standing in the doorway to what was most likely his bedroom. He was dressed like Karim, in the robes of his forefathers, but without the encompassing headdress. The combination of East and West was doubly disturbing, and Abby glanced about her nervously, wondering exactly what Rachid's intentions were.

'They told me you were ill,' she said now,

summoning all the anger and resentment she could gather, and he inclined his head in silent assent.

'Karim!' He snapped his fingers in sharp dismissal, and after the servant had left them he went on: 'It is true. I have been unwell. Something I ate, perhaps.'

Abby was still suspicious. 'You look all right to me,' she retorted, pushing her hands into the pockets of her sheepskin jacket, ignoring the fact that he did look a little pale. 'In any case, you're not incapacitated. You could have come downstairs.'

Rachid straightened from the lounging position he had adopted and came fully into the room. 'I was advised to rest,' he replied quietly. 'And as I did not wish to postpone your visit, I saw no reason why we should not enjoy our meal here.'

Abby pressed her lips together. 'I'd rather not. I think it would be better if we arranged another meeting, at another time. At the solicitor's, perhaps.'

Rachid's lips thinned. 'What is wrong with us sharing a meal here? Have we not done so many times before?'

'That was different.'

'How different?'

Abby hunched her shoulders. 'We—we were married—'

'We are still married,' he snapped shortly. 'And if you wish me to treat this matter favourably, then I suggest you stop putting obstacles in my way.'

Abby looked reluctantly at him. 'Are you going to dress?'

'I am dressed,' he retorted, controlling his temper with difficulty. 'Now—please, take off your coat, and I will offer you a drink.'

Abby shrugged, and then complied. It was easier than allowing him to help her, easier than feeling those long brown fingers brush her neck or bring a tingle to the sensitive bones of her shoulders. She dropped the sheepskin jacket on to a chair by the door, and then stood apprehensively in the middle of the floor, aware of his eyes moving over her. She was wearing boots, her pants zipped inside their soft suede lining, accentuating the masculine stance she adopted, and with a faint quirk of his eyebrows he crossed the floor on silent feet.

'Martini, sherry? Or something stronger?' he queried, waiting for her decision, and she deliberately chose Scotch. She needed something to combat the feelings of inadequacy he aroused inside her, and it gave her a sense of reassurance to have a glass in her hand.

He poured the whisky without comment, dropping in several cubes of ice at her instigation, and then carried the glass back to her. Abby took it cautiously, taking care not to touch his fingers, and he watched her sip its contents with a strangely enigmatic smile.

'Aren't you having anything?' she enquired, selfconscious in spite of her assumed arrogance, and with a shrug Rachid returned to the tray resting on a cabinet near the long windows. He poured himself a small glass of orange juice, and raised it in a silent toast before swallowing the sun-kissed liquid, and Abby's nerves tightened anew at this deliberate exhibition of abstemiousness.

'Will you not sit down?'

He indicated a low sofa, and although Abby would have preferred a chair, she refused to let him think she was afraid of him. She subsided on to the striped cushions, albeit rather stiffly, and crossing her legs rested her arm holding the glass across her knees.

Rachid studied her for a moment, then he went to summon Karim once more. 'We will eat now,' he advised shortly, giving his instructions, and Karim withdrew with his usual gesture of obeisance.

'I understand you have resumed your position as Daley's secretary,' Rachid commented, as they waited for the food, and Abby nodded. 'How convenient that he needed a secretary at just this time.'

Abby glanced quickly up at him. 'It wasn't arranged, if that's what you think. Brad had had a series of girls since I left, none of them satisfactory. He dismissed the last one the week before I returned to London.'

Rachid's lips curled. 'Is that what he told you?'

'It's true.'

'It is true that Daley had had several different girls working for him, but I find the latter part of your statement hard to believe. I think he dismissed his last secretary because he knew you were returning to London. He knew that working for him you would feel more loyalty than for some strange employer, who has not had time to win your confidence.'

'What do you mean?'

Rachid flexed his shoulder muscles wearily. 'I mean that your estimable boss knew I was looking for you, and was determined to put as many obstacles in my way as possible.'

Abby gasped. 'That's ridiculous! What could it achieve?'

'It could make the difference between your staying in London, or returning to Abarein.'

'No!'

'Yes.' He was inflexible. 'By restoring the—what do you say? Status quo?—Daley knew you would think twice before making a decision in my favour. Whereas,' he made an eloquent gesture, 'in a strange job, with a strange employer, and perhaps not entirely happy. . .' he spread his hands, 'you might have weighed the consequences more—wisely.'

Abby drew a short breath. 'If you're implying that having a good job has anything to do with my decision, you couldn't be more wrong. I—I wouldn't go back with you whatever the circumstances.'

Karim's arrival with the food forestalled any further discussion at that point, and he wheeled the trolley into the room, laden down with an assortment of dishes. The sides of the trolley opened out to provide a comfortably-sized table for two, and after laying out the cutlery and uncorking the wine, Rachid dismissed him.

'We will serve ourselves,' he told the man curtly, in Arabic, and Abby was amazed at how easily she followed their exchange. Languages were like that, she thought, once learned, never forgotten.

Karim had placed two of the upright chairs at either side of the improvised table, and Abby took the one Rachid offered with polite acquiescence. Her husband seated himself opposite, and then asked her what she would like of the various foods provided.

Abby looked at the table rather perplexedly. There was a bewildering choice of dishes, and in her present state of nervousness she found all of them a little overpowering. Egyptian caviare was rich and salty, luscious pink prawns nestled on a bed of tossed salad, a thick yoghurt was coiled creamily in a chilled dish, and a steaming *bisque* simmered over a tiny flame.

And they were only appetizers, she thought unhappily. To follow there was a choice of Middle Eastern dishes like kebabs, and a thick soup served with vegetables called *moulukhiya*, and more traditionally Western foods like steak, and lamb chops, and tiny whole ducklings, served with orange sauce. Obviously Karim had been instructed to provide a variety of choice, and Abby was overwhelmed by it.

'What will you have?'

Rachid was looking enquiringly at her now, and Abby made a helpless gesture. 'I'm not sure. There's so many things. It—it's hard to decide.'

'Then have a little of each,' suggested Rachid dryly, indicating the caviare. 'I can recommend this, although perhaps you would prefer something sweeter.'

'I—no. The caviare would be fine,' murmured Abby uncomfortably, reaching for a cracker, and while Rachid served her, she gazed with wonder at the enormous bowl of strawberries just visible on a lower shelf, and the juicy figs beside a tray of cheeses.

Despite her misgivings, the food was so excellent that Abby made a good meal, following the caviare with kebabs, and finishing with strawberries and cream. Rachid, she noticed, ate next to nothing, and as the meal progressed, she wondered if she had not been a little insensitive about his illness. It was obvious the food had no interest for him, and she felt slightly ashamed when he had gone to so much trouble to offer her so many delicious things.

'That was—marvellous,' she said at last, finishing the wine in her glass, and refusing his offer of more. 'I didn't realise I was so hungry. I'm sorry you couldn't enjoy it with me.'

Rachid pushed his chair away from the table and stood up. 'I am glad you are pleased,' he remarked, summoning Karim once more. 'We will have coffee now, I think. Then we can talk.'

Abby nodded, leaving the table herself as the swarthy manservant appeared, wandering restlessly about the room as he wheeled the trolley away, examining the pictures on the walls. Rachid's words about talking had reminded her of her reasons for being here, and while she had not forgotten the outcome of this meeting, she was not looking forward to their proposed discussion.

Karim had the coffee prepared and waiting for

them, and after it was served Rachid asked that
he should not disturb them again. 'I will ring if
there is anything else I need,' he instructed in
their own language, and Karim retired with a
gesture of understanding.

Alone with Rachid, Abby could feel her nerves
tightening, as much from an awareness of her
own weakness as from any fear of their isolation.
Her husband was still a most disturbingly attractive man, and she was woman enough to respond
to his vulnerability. His pallor now was not con-
trived, and although she despised his treatment
of her in the past, she could not help the feelings
of sympathy he aroused inside her. But they were
feelings which had to be controlled, she acknowledged, half afraid they might arouse a physical
response that would be wholly self-destructive.

When she made no move to sit down beside
the tray Karim had provided, Rachid gained her
permission to seek respite on the couch she had
occupied earlier.

'You must forgive me,' he said, running a
weary hand over his temples. 'I feel so stupidly
weak, and I am not very good company.'

Abby pressed her lips together, walking back
to the couch with reluctant concern. 'You should
have phoned,' she said, with an offhand gesture,
seating herself on the very edge of the cushions,
half turned towards him. 'But don't let it worry
you, this is hardly a social occasion, is it?'

Rachid rested his head back against the satin
upholstery, viewing her thoughtfully. 'It is in your
favour, is it not?' he remarked, his dark eyes
heavy-lidded and intense. 'Everything is in your

favour, and I have no more weapons with which to fight you.'

Abby took charge of the coffee pot, pouring two cups, and when he shook his head, taking hers into her hands. 'Don't be dramatic, Rachid,' she exclaimed, nervously tasting the scalding liquid. 'It's not a battle we're conducting, or at least it shouldn't be. Why can't we behave calmly and civilly, like adults, not children? Treat one another with courtesy and respect—'

'Because I do not feel very courteous or respectful!' he retorted harshly, his hand suddenly reaching out and imprisoning her wrist. 'I feel angry, and aggrieved, and not a little insane at the thought of your breaking up our marriage—' his fingers tightened, '—and maybe sharing the intimacies we have shared with someone—'

His words broke off at Abby's sudden cry. The unexpectedness of his action had caught her unawares, but it was her own instinctive withdrawal which had caused what happened next. Her jerky attempt to escape him sent the fragile cup tumbling into her lap, spilling its contents over her velvet pants. The hot liquid was quickly absorbed and her thighs stung painfully as the fiery cloth clung to them.

'In the name of Allah!'

As Abby struggled to her feet, Rachid rose also, thrusting her plucking hands aside and reaching purposefully for the buttons that fastened at her waist. With little care for the expensive cut of the pants, he tore the fastening apart and ignoring her frantic attempts to prevent him, he determinedly pushed the offending garment down to her knees.

It was a tremendous relief to feel the air against her burning thighs, but humiliation overcame all other emotions. Even the pain of her scalded flesh was not sufficient compensation for standing there in her underwear, with Rachid's dark eyes running impatiently over her. With a sob of frustration she turned aside, groping for the trousers in total ignominy.

'Do not cover them again,' grated Rachid roughly, grasping her arm and turning her back to face him. His eyes lowered to the revealing welts of scarlet flesh, and he uttered an oath. 'Come—they need to be treated,' he added, indicating the door into his bedroom. 'Karin keeps some medication in the bathroom. I will attend to them myself.'

'No!' Abby pulled her arm away from his grasp, trying desperately to cover herself. 'I—I'll go. I can't stay like this. We—we'll have to arrange another meeting.'

'Do not be a fool!' he snapped, squatting down before her and touching the throbbing flesh with cool, probing fingers. 'I have some cream which will take all the heat out of this. Have the goodness to let me make amends for my carelessness.'

Abby's mouth was dry from her unwilling response to his touch. It was so long since she had felt his fingers against her skin, and the unguarded emotions of the last few minutes had left her dangerously susceptible. 'It—it wasn't your fault,' she got out chokingly, trying to push his hands aside. 'I shouldn't have—have jumped like that. It was a stupid thing to do.'

'So—let me put it right for you,' he said,

unzipping her boots before she could prevent him, and straightening once more. 'Take off your trousers and I will have Karim take them to be sponged and pressed. By the time you are ready to leave they will be dry.'

Abby made a helpless gesture. 'Oh, very well. Do you—do you have something I can wear?'

'Well, not trousers, I regret,' he responded shortly, as she fumbled to remove the pants, and then held them protectively in front of her. Then, irritably: 'But why do you act like this? As if I had not seen you this way many times before? As if I did not know your body almost as well as I know my own?'

Abby merely pressed the garment closer to her. 'You said you had something I could wear,' she reminded him tightly, and with an impatient shrug he led the way into the bedroom.

Like the sitting room, it was large and high-ceilinged, with a king-sized double bed, and a soft beige carpet underfoot. There were high tall-boys, and lots of fitted cupboards, and plenty of mirrors with which to view oneself from every angle. Abby doubted Rachid was aware of them. Whatever else he was, he was not vain, but they made her acutely aware of her ridiculous appearance, and she longed to hide the pale slender length of her legs.

Rachid extracted a dressing gown from his wardrobe. It was made of dark blue silk and would obviously be too long for her, but at least it would cover her, and Abby took it gratefully.

'There are splashes of coffee on your jacket, too,' Rachid pointed out as he handed the dressing gown to her. 'I would suggest you send the whole outfit for sponging, except that you might misconstrue my motives.'

Abby hesitated a moment, and then turning her back on him she quickly removed the jacket, too. With the folds of the dressing gown securely about her, she felt more able to face him, and with a mildly sardonic grimace he gathered the suit and went out of the room.

Karim was obviously never far away from his master, and it took little time for Rachid to despatch him about his business. Waiting for the servant to depart, Abby was somewhat taken aback when Rachid came back into the bedroom, but meeting her puzzled apprehension, he quickly explained his purpose.

'The cream is in the bathroom,' he declared, crossing to another door. 'If you will expose the burns, I will deal with them.'

Abby sighed. She was tempted to say there was no need, that since the cloth had been removed so swiftly the damage done had been slight, and was already cooling of its own accord. But Rachid had already disappeared into the bathroom, and loath to increase the intimacy of the situation, she determinedly went back into the sitting room.

She was perched on the sofa when Rachid reappeared, and his eyes narrowed at her obvious efforts to sustain her detachment. She had exposed only one leg to his gaze, and the lower half of that was wrapped around with blue silk.

Shrugging, he knelt before her, unscrewing the cap of the tube of cream in his hands and squeezing a little of the white substance into his palm.

Then firmly and deliberately, he applied the
cream to the inflamed flesh, moving his palm
gently and rhythmically over its sensitised
surface.

It was amazing how soothing the cream was,
Abby thought, feeling all the heat leaving the
lesion. As he continued to massage it into the
skin, she could feel the taut flesh softening, and
its dryness was replaced with regenerative oils.
But it wasn't just the cream that was inducing
this feeling of well-being inside her. It was the
cool hardness of Rachid's hands that brought a
sensuous lethargy, and caused her convulsive
hold on the robe to be released, exposing her
slender limbs with reckless abandon.

Rachid said nothing, however. He merely
transferred his ministrations to her other leg, and
presently both injuries had been similarly treated.
Then he got to his feet again, recapping the tube
and returning it to its place in the bathroom.

She heard the taps running as he washed his
hands, and the everyday sound dispelled the feelings of inertia which had gripped her. Hastily she
came upright on the sofa, gathering her splayed
legs, and wrapping the gown about her once more.
She hardly liked to think what Rachid must have
thought of her abandoned pose, and her cheeks
burned as he came back into the room.

'Er—thank you,' she murmured awkwardly,
realising some response was in order, but he
merely quirked an eyebrow.

'They feel better now?' he enquired, his eyes
probing the tightly draped folds, and she nodded
quickly, hoping he would not ask to see.

'Good.'

He dropped down on to the sofa beside her once more, and as he did so, she saw how fatigued he looked. His illness, whatever it was, must be more serious than she had thought, and the prolonged exertion had exhausted him.

'Are you feeling sick?' she asked, as he expelled his breath on a sigh, and slumped against the cushions. 'You look—awful! Ought you to be in bed?'

Rachid shook his head wearily. 'I am all right,' he assured her firmly. 'Just a mild indisposition, as I said. Now, shall we continue our conversation? You were saying something about—being civilised.'

Abby shook her head. 'Rachid, I think you should be in bed. We can talk some other time.' She glanced at him anxiously. 'I can easily wait for Karim, and—'

'No!' His denial was harsh and determined. 'We will talk now. I want to know what you intend to do. If you refuse to return to Abarein, will you be staying in London?'

Abby bent her head. 'Probably.' She moved her shoulders awkwardly. 'Does it matter? Once we're divorced—'

'And if I refuse,' he overrode her grimly. 'If I refuse to give you a divorce, what then?'

'You couldn't do that, Rachid,' she said quietly, avoiding his eyes. 'In England it's possible to get a divorce without the consent of both parties—'

'In Abarein you would still be my wife.'

'That would be foolish, Rachid!' She looked

at him now, finding refuge in impatience. 'You
know perfectly well your father will welcome
this solution. He'll waste no time in finding you
another wife—'

'I do not want another wife,' retorted Rachid
roughly. 'I want you!'

'No—' Abbey recoiled from the passion in his
eyes. 'Rachid, you're not being reasonable—'

'I do not feel reasonable!' he grated thickly,
his hands clenching on his knees.

His face was very pale now, and there were
beads of perspiration standing on his forehead,
that gave his skin an unhealthy sheen. Abby
guessed that the strain of their altercation was
draining his strength, but although compassion
urged her to reassure him, the small grip she still
had on common sense argued the illogicality of
giving in to him, just because he was not well!.

'Is there something I can do?' she offered, feeling obliged to say something. 'Is there anything
I can get you?'

'You know what I want,' he said savagely,
levering himself up from the cushions, but even
as he spoke his gaze seemed to falter. One second
he was looking at her with smouldering animosity, and the next a curiously glazed expression
had taken its place. 'You know what I want,' he
repeated, in an odd monotone, and then his eyes
closed completely, and his body sagged.

Abby was shocked. Just for a moment—*a fleeting moment*—she wondered if he might be
fooling her, but one touch of his icy flesh assured
her that this was not so. He had lost conscious-
ness, and she hadn't the faintest idea what to do.

Getting to her feet, she looked round desperately for the bell. Karim couldn't be far away, she thought with relief, and then turned back to the couch, when Rachid started to speak again.

'What are you doing?' he protested, his voice returning to its previous tenor. 'Come and sit down again, and stop looking so anxious. You have nothing to fear from me.'

Abby's eyes alighted on the bell, and trying not to make her actions too obvious, she backed away from the sofa. 'You—you passed out,' she said, explaining her dilemma. 'I'll get Karim to come and put you to bed.'

'I am not a child,' he muttered, getting unsteadily to his feet at her words. 'Have the decency not to treat me as one. I am quite capable of putting myself to bed, as and when it is necessary. And if my behaviour frightens you, then calm yourself. Have you never seen anyone with malaria before?'

Abby's lips parted. 'Malaria?'

'A similar disease,' he confirmed, taking a few uncertain steps across the room. 'It is an annoyance, nothing more. By tomorrow I shall be completely recovered.'

Abby watched his uneven progress towards the bedroom door, and then, unable to resist the need to help him, she went and put an arm around his waist, encouraging him to support himself with an arm across her shoulders. For an instant he held back from her, but then, weakened by the effort, he allowed her to help him into the bedroom.

He sat on the end of the bed while she folded

back the covers, and then sprawled wearily between the sheets. With his head upon the pillows, he looked up at her with heavy eyes, and it was all she could do not to smooth the dark hair back from his forehead.

'Do you want me to get Karim to undress you?' she asked, viewing his heavy robe with some misgivings, and he stretched out a hand to warm his palm against her cheek.

She flinched away from him then, but his fingers curved around her nape, imprisoning her above him, and his eyes were perfectly lucid as they met her startled gaze.

'Will you help me?' he asked, resisting her efforts to release herself, and her breathing quickened at his unconscious sensuality.

'Rachid, I can't. . .' she got out unsteadily, feeling the strength of his magnetic attraction. Relaxed upon the pillows, he had an overwhelming sexuality, and she would not have been human if she had not responded to it. 'Please, let me go, Rachid. You said I had nothing to fear from you.'

'That is so.' His fingers relaxed their hold and his arm fell to the bed. 'I cannot force you to help me. I merely thought that our past relationship might mean something to you. So be it! Ring for Karim. He is not so churlish.'

'Rachid. . .'

Abby stared down at him helplessly, and then, with definite reservations, she unfastened the cord of his robe. It fell apart revealing the plain tunic beneath, and with his assistance she removed both garments. It necessitated her kneeling on the bed, and she was sweating by the time he was naked.

Ignoring the masculine scent of his body, she tucked the covers around him, and then stood hesitantly beside the bed, waiting for his dismissal.

'Thank you,' he said, turning his face against the pillows. 'I am grateful.'

'I'll wait until Karim brings my clothes and then I'll go,' she offered, as he closed his eyes, but Rachid did not answer her, and with a feeling of helplessness, Abby left him alone.

In the living room, she examined her reflection with some dissatisfaction. Her exertions on Rachid's behalf had loosened her knot of hair, and it was presently hanging in tendrils about her neck. Tugging out the hairpins, she allowed it to tumble to her waist, then rummaged in her bag for a comb to restore it to order.

It was while she was combing her hair that she heard Rachid's voice again. Thinking he was calling her, she opened the door to his bedroom, hesitating on the threshold, unwilling to intrude if she had been mistaken.

He was talking, it was true, but not to her. In the light from the lamp she had left burning, she could see him tossing and turning on his pillows, muttering to himself, in the throes of delirium. He had pushed the enveloping covers down to his waist, and the moist expanse of his chest was exposed, brown and muscular, and finely covered with dark hair.

Putting down her comb, Abby advanced into the room, drawing the covers up about him, and running an anxious hand over his forehead. Where before he had been chilled, now he was burning up, and she wondered if she ought to summon Karim after all.

'Abby!'

While she stood there pondering the best course of action, Rachid's eyes had opened, and now he was looking at her with only slightly opaque pupils.

'Rachid?' she murmured, coming close to the bed and allowing a slight smile of encouragement to lift her lips. 'How are you feeling? You're very hot?'

'Am I?' He moved restlessly. 'I feel cold. Did you open a window?'

'You can't open windows here,' Abby explained gently. 'They're all double-glazed. And the air-conditioning's on seventy.'

'It is?' His brows drew together, and he hunched his shoulders. 'I am so cold.' He withdrew a hand from the covers and held it out to her. 'Come and keep me warm, Abby. I need you.'

Abby was staggered, but she tried not to show it. 'You know I can't do that,' she replied reasonably. 'I can get you an electric blanket—'

'I do not want an electric blanket,' he snapped, levering himself up on his elbows. 'Abby. . .' The dark eyes glazed. 'Abby, do not leave me. Please! I beg of you!'

'Rachid—'

Abby was caught in the trap of her own emotions. She couldn't stay with him, she couldn't, she thought wildly, but the trouble was, she couldn't leave him either.

'Rachid, try to be sensible—'

'Come here!'

She was afraid he might get out of bed and come after her if she did not obey him, and with a sense of helplessness she allowed her fingers to be enclosed by his.

'Abby, Abby. . .' He sank back against the pillows with her fingers to his lips, his tongue finding her palm with bone-melting intimacy. 'Get into bed,' he murmured huskily, finding the sensitive veins on the inner side of her wrist. 'I want to hold you in my arms.'

'Rachid, I can't,' she protested, but inside, a small wicked voice was urging: *Why not? Why not? What have you got to lose?*

'Why not?' Rachid demanded now, his eyes dark with emotion. 'You are my wife, are you not? My woman. Would you deny your husband that which is his by holy law?'

This was rapidly getting out of hand. Abby silenced the voice inside her, and said sharply: 'I don't know what your game is, Rachid, but I have to go—'

'Go? Go? Where would you go?' His gaze was blank with incomprehension. 'Your place is here, with me. Would you desert me when I need you most?'

'Rachid—'

Abby was attempting to free herself when a light tap sounded at the door. She guessed it was Karim, returning with her suit, and with a desperate glance over her shoulder she pulled her hand away.

Trying to ignore Rachid's weak recriminations, she crossed the living room and hastened to open the door. The manservant stood waiting patiently, her suit folded over his arm, but his eyes moved past her to the open door of the bedroom beyond, and their instinctive anxiety encouraged Abby to confide in him.

'The Prince is not well,' she explained, flushing as the man's enquiring gaze reminded her of her earlier scepticism. 'Has he seen a doctor recently? He seems very feverish. Is there no medication he could take?'

Karim bowed. 'My master was visited by a doctor before you came, mistress.' His lips tightened. 'It is through his work with the children at the mission that he has contracted the fever, but I am assured that the drug the doctor gave him will cure him as before.'

Abby blinked. 'His work—at the mission?' she was confused.

'Yes, mistress.' Karim's expression was disapproving. 'My master insists on using his skill as a teacher to help those less fortunate than himself. Regrettably, he will not listen to reason.'

Abby glanced behind her. It was obvious that Karim was not in favour of Rachid laying himself open to disease in the poorer sections of Xanthia, but it was untypical of her husband, she would have thought, not to care about his own welfare.

With a shrug, she turned back to the manservant. 'He has been given quinine, I suppose,' she asked, and Karim nodded.

'You will stay with him, mistress?' he suggested, his dark brows arched in silent admonition, and although Abby wanted to deny it, she found she couldn't.

'For—for a while, perhaps,' she agreed unwill-

ingly, taking the velvet pants and jacket from
him. 'I'll call you when I need a cab. In an hour,
perhaps?'

Karim's face was expressionless now. 'If you
say so, mistress,' he essayed politely, and with a
faint bow of his head, he withdrew.

Back in the bedroom, Abby found to her horror
that Rachid was out of bed and fumbling
impatiently for his clothes. Her pulses raced at
the sight of his lean, brown body, but ignoring
the intimacies of the situation, she went swiftly
towards him, her voice firm and authoritative.

'Come along,' she said, sustaining the imper-
sonality, folding back the bedcovers with one
hand and helping to support him with the other.
'You must rest. You'll feel better in the morning.
I'll stay until you go to sleep, and then you can
ring me when you've recovered.'

Rachid resisted her efforts to subdue him, however. 'Hmm, Abby, your hair smells delicious,'
he murmured, turning his mouth against her
temple, and instead of pushing him back against
the covers, she found herself in his arms.

'Rachid, please. . .'

She twisted recklessly, trying to avoid his
searching lips. His arms seemed amazingly strong
after his previous debility, and crushed against
his warm body, she was overwhelmingly aware
of her own weakness. Somehow she had to get
away from him, but the longer he held her the
more difficult it was going to be.

'Abby, soul of my soul, stop fighting me,' he
muttered roughly, holding her closer. 'You do not

really want to leave me, do you? Not when I can make you feel like this—'

Her protests died beneath the hungry pressure of his mouth, and her resistance was a small thing against his superior strength. Besides, when his lips parted hers, she felt herself melting beneath their probing caress, and her overheated blood spilled like fire along her veins. His hands were at her waist, releasing the cord of his dressing gown, and she tore her mouth from his as he found the swelling warmth of her body.

'Rachid, don't do this—' she choked, as her skin tingled with the expectation of his touch, but his emotions had taken over, and she doubted that he heard her.

He compelled her down on to the bed, covering her trembling limbs with his, stroking the tears from her cheek with a tender finger. He was infinitely gentle, infinitely loving, and gradually her opposition gave way to a tentative response. If the voice that had previously urged her to accept him now permitted itself a contemptuous sneer at her surrender, she refused to listen, and the exploring sensuality of his caress drove all coherent thought from her mind. She was sinking into a well of emotion, an abyss of feeling, where all that mattered was that Rachid should go on holding her, and kissing her, and arousing her to the explosive heights only he could achieve.

His mouth moved knowingly against hers, demanding and taking with hungry adandon. As his kiss hardened, so too did his demands upon her, and she yielded completely to his passion, arching against him with involuntary eagerness.

Her hands spread against the smooth skin of his shoulders, her nails curving into the flesh, and then softening again as his mouth lowered to the swollen fullness of her breasts. He teased their peaks with an enticing tongue, and then possessed their hardened upsurge with his lips.

By the time he sought the ultimate invasion of her senses, Abby was desperate for his possession, uncaring of the consequences of her actions, inflamed by emotions too strong to deny. She wanted Rachid, she wanted to feel him a part of her, and most of all she wanted the satisfaction only he could give her. . .

CHAPTER FIVE

RACHID was asleep when Abby left the suite. He had fallen into an exhausted slumber immediately after their lovemaking, and she guessed the exertion had achieved what drugs could not. He was resting, and at peace, and sleep would perform its miracle of recovery.

For Abby, however, there was no such miracle, no such recovery. Dressing in the semi-darkness of the bedroom, fumbling over hooks and buttons, she felt only disgust at her behaviour, and contempt for the weakness Rachid had found so easy to exploit. She had known what he was like before she came here, she reviled herself bitterly, she had suspected the loathesome vulnerability of her body. Yet she had succumbed to his passion with only a token protest, and how could she blame him when her strength should have been greater than his?

It was an irony she would have to live with, that no matter how much she despised her husband and his failings, where he was concerned she had her own Achilles heel. In truth, it might not have happened if he had not appealed to her sympathies, but nothing could alter the fact that physically he still had the power to arouse her.

It deepened the sense of injustice she felt towards him to know that for the first time since she left Abarein she had been forced to an awareness of her own femininity. She didn't want to be reminded of that, and all the humiliation it involved, and she felt violently sick at the recollection of those months of uncertainty. She was free of that now, she told herself fiercely, free of marriage and all it entailed. This was the end, it was over, *over*. And if she saw Rachid again, she would make sure he understood she meant what she said.

It was after two a.m. when she let herself into the house in Dacre Mews. She had not summoned Karim, but had asked the night porter to call her a cab, and she felt raw and weary as she climbed the stairs to her room. Where now the competent career woman? she chided herself contemptuously, as she took off her clothes. What had happened to the rampant feminist, with her high ideals and controlled emotions? As the lamplight picked out the rosy marks of Rachid's possession upon her, with her limbs aching from the hungry passion of his lovemaking, she acknowledged the inherent weakness of the female character, that she had to fight if she ever wanted to respect herself again.

The opportunity to tell her father where she had been the previous evening came rather sooner than she would have liked. She was sitting hunched over her second cup of coffee the following morning when he came into the kitchen-cum-breakfast room, and helping himself to some toast, seated himself opposite her.

'You were late last night,' he commented, spreading a thin layer of butter on his bread before reaching for the marmalade. 'You didn't tell me you were going out.'

Abby hesitated, and then put down her cup. 'As a matter of fact, I had dinner with Rachid,' she admitted flatly. And at her father's raised brows: 'But don't get the wrong idea. It was only to discuss the divorce.'

'I see.' Professor Gillespie regarded his daughter's pale face with some misgivings. 'And did you? Talk about the divorce, I mean?'

'Of course.' Abby's response was too quick, and she hastily qualified it. 'That is—we didn't exactly go into details.' She sighed, reluctant to go on, and yet feeling compelled to do so. 'Rachid was ill. He's contracted malaria, and two nights ago he had an attack.'

'Two nights ago?' echoed her father. 'You mean, after he left here?'

'Apparently.' Abby moved her shoulders off-handedly. 'It's not serious. Karim—that's Rachid's manservant—he said he'd had treatment.'

'And was last night's meeting a spur-of-the-moment decision?' enquired Professor Gillespie quietly. 'Couldn't you have postponed it?'

'If I'd known, I suppose so,' Abby shrugged.

'I take it then it was arranged while Rachid was here?'

'Yes. Oh, I know I should have told you, but—' Abby got up from her stool, 'I didn't want you to think that—well, that we might get back together again.'

'And you won't?'

'No.' Abby reached for her coat which she had

draped casually over the radiator on the corner. 'I've told you, Dad. We should never have got married. Our—our values are different.'

'But you seemed so much in love. . .' protested her father, urgently. 'Abby, Rachid's intentions are good—'

Abby's laugh was short and mirthless. 'What is it they say about good intentions—that the road to hell is paved with them?'

'You're very hard, Abby.'

Hard? Abby's lips quivered for a moment. If he only knew! she thought bitterly. He wouldn't call her hard. He would realise how stupidly soft she was!

Liz Forster rang during the course of the morning. She didn't usually ring Abby at work, but her first words indicated her reasons for doing so.

'I expected you to ring me,' she said, half reproachfully, 'but I hear you've been too busy to bother about old friends.'

Abby's nails curled into her palms. 'Where did you hear that?'

'Oh—around, darling. Isn't it true?'

Abby hesitated. 'It depends what you've heard.'

Liz sounded impatient. 'Don't be obtuse, darling. I mean Rachid, and you know it. You were seen entering his hotel yesterday evening, and from what I hear, you didn't eat in the dining room.'

Abby sighed. 'Honestly, Liz—'

'Now don't go getting all uptight about it. Your secret's safe with me. Unfortunately, there are others in the agency who are less scrupulous.'

'You mean someone else saw me?'

'Just Damon,' responded Liz half maliciously. 'I know it must be a source of annoyance to you, but he had had a meeting with your inestimable husband that had had to be cancelled because he was—how did they put it?—indisposed?'

Abby felt exasperation gnawing at her nerves. 'Well, as it happens, it's true,' she conceded, realising she would get no peace unless Liz was satisfied. 'Rachid was—unwell.'

'But not unwell enough not to see you.'

Abby bit her lip. 'I suppose not.'

'So what happened?' Liz was growing irritated. 'Do I have to drag every detail out of you? I thought we were friends. My goodness, the fuss you made about seeing him Tuesday night, I thought the last thing I would hear was that you were actually having dinner with him at his hotel!'

Abby expelled her breath heavily. 'It wasn't like that.' She struggled for inspiration. 'We—it was a meeting arranged to discuss our divorce, that's all.'

'But you did speak to him on Tuesday night?'

'As he was waiting for me outside, which you must know very well, I could hardly avoid it,' retorted Abby heatedly and Liz made a sound of apology.

'You do understand how I was placed, don't you?' she pleaded, cajolingly. 'I mean, when Damon asked, what could I say?'

Abby's head was beginning to ache. 'It doesn't matter now, Liz. It's over. I—well, I've got to go. Brad wants these letters typing by lunchtime, and it's getting late.'

'All right, darling.' Liz was sympathetic. 'Give me a ring in a couple of days. We could meet for lunch or something. After Rachid has gone back to Abarein.'

'Good idea,' Abby agreed, grateful for the respite. 'See you soon.'

'Sure thing,' Liz answered eagerly, and Abby replaced her receiver.

Yet, in spite of her comparatively easy exchange with the other girl, for the rest of the morning Abby found herself wishing she had not admitted that she and Rachid were discussing divorce. It wasn't that it wasn't true, it was just that Liz did work for a news agency, and information like that was solid gold.

She had lunch in the staff canteen. A bowl of soup and a cup of coffee were all that she could stomach, and she returned to her office feeling utterly dejected. The aftermath of the previous nights' events was beginning to take its toll on her, and depression deepened the feelings of guilt and self-deprecation she nurtured.

She entered her office wearily, head bent to extract the key of her desk from her handbag, and then halted aghast at the sight of her husband lounging familiarly in her chair, his feet raised to rest comfortably on the end of her desk.

He still looked pale, but the unhealthy fever-ishness had left him, and in its place was a hard implacability that sent ripples of apprehension tingling along her spine. At her appearance he swung his feet to the floor and stood up, tall and forbidding in the dark leather car coat he was wearing. She found it incredibly difficult to believe that only the night before he had been trembling in her arms, and yet when she met his smouldering gaze it was not impossible to remember his unleashed passion.

'Abby!' He greeted her politely, the slight bow of his head reminiscent of Karim, but his manner in no way resembled that of an inferior. 'I have been waiting for you.'

'Have you?' Abby's clipped words were indicative of her instinctive withdrawal. 'I'm sorry, I didn't realise you had an appointment.'

'An appointment?' For a moment his jaw hardened in response to the implied insult, but then he controlled himself again, and said quietly: 'Why did you walk out on me, Abby? It was not very kind. We still have a lot more to say to one another.'

'Really?' Abby's tone was deliberately off-hand, as she put the width of the desk between them. 'I should have thought last night said it all. At least, it's shown me that I was a fool to trust you.'

'What do you mean?' His voice was raised, but then, as if realising that there might be people in the surrounding offices who could overhear their conversation, he spoke more levelly. 'Surely last night must have convinced you that we belong together, that we have wasted so much time by staying apart?'

Abby gasped. 'You really mean that? You think because—because we went to bed together that—that I'll be persuaded to come back to you?'

'Abby, be reasonable—'

'No, you be reasonable!' Her eyes flashed. 'You took advantage of me, whatever way you look at it. All right, I know you were feverish, that perhaps you wouldn't have acted as you did if I hadn't felt foolishly sorry for you—'

'*Sorry for me*!' Rachid circled the desk with a threatening tread, his dark attire accentuating his Arab ancestry. 'Do you pretend you allowed me to make love to you because you were *sorry for me*! You wanted me, Abby, just as much as I wanted you, and feeling sorry for me had nothing to do with it!'

'That's not true.' Abby backed away from him. 'I did feel sorry for you. Why else did I stay? Ask Karim. He asked me to keep you company.' She licked her dry lips. 'And you took advantage of that.'

'You little—' Rachid bit off an expletive, his dark eyes glittering dangerously. 'Do you mean to tell me that last night meant nothing to you? Nothing at all?'

'It proved that you'll use any method, any method at all to humiliate me!' she flung at him tautly, the wall at her back preventing any further withdrawal from him. 'Perhaps you weren't ill, perhaps that was just a ploy to get me into the bedroom—'

'Be silent!' His hand crushed the words on her lips, and his mouth was a thin hard line. Then he shook his head half incredulously, staring into the shadowy purple irises that met his gaze so fearfully. 'I do not believe this,' he said, his voice low and thick with emotion. 'I will not accept that you merely responded to a given stimulus. You were with me, Abby, every step of the way, and what is more, I have the scars to prove it!'

Abby choked on his hand, tearing his fingers aside, and feeling the well of nausea in her throat. 'That's a filthy thing to say!' she exclaimed, turning aside from him as the muscles of her throat demanded release, and the spasm of coughing that gripped her successfully evaded his angry retort. By the time she recovered, Rachid had himself in control again, and was turning away towards the door.

'It is obvious you refuse to face facts,' he said harshly, supporting himself against the door frame. 'I had hoped that—but never mind. I can see I am wasting my time. You obviously want your freedom more than you want me. So be it.' He moved his shoulders in a weary, defeated gesture. '*Saida!*'

Abby heard his footsteps receding down the corridor, and then she sank down at her desk, her legs shaking so much they would not support her. He had gone. *He had gone!* It should be a relief. But it wasn't. Resting her elbows on the desk, she buried her face in her hands. Dear God, she couldn't love him after the way he had treated her, could she? But if she didn't, what was this terrible emotion that was tearing her apart?

'*Abby!*'

Brad's anxious voice broke into her tormented reverie, and with a startled jerk of her shoulders she quickly took refuge in blowing her nose on a tissue from the box she kept on her desk. She guessed it must be fifteen minutes since Rachid departed, and her emotional outburst had left her eyes red and puffy and hopelessly revealing.

'I—I must be getting a cold,' she mumbled, hoping Brad would take the hint and leave her, but he didn't; he leant over the desk and lifted her chin, his expression hardening as it took in the evident marks of her tears.

'In God's name, what's been happening here?' he demanded angrily. 'Who's done this to you? Just tell me and—'

'Nobody's done anything to me, Brad,' she protested, pulling herself away from him. 'I just felt—depressed, that's all.'

Brad gave her a sceptical look. 'Pull the other one,' he retorted shortly. 'It's Rachid, isn't it? I should have guessed. When I spoke to you the other morning I knew that something was wrong, but it didn't immediately occur to me that your ex-husband might be in town.'

'He's not my *ex*-husband,' replied Abby pragmatically, and then flushed beneath Brad's cynical appraisal. 'Well, it's true! If he was, it might be easier.'

'You mean he's making a nuisance of himself?'

Abby sniffed. *Making a nuisance of himself!* That must be the understatement of the year.

'Oh, you know Rachid,' she said now, blowing her nose again. 'He doesn't like to think I have a mind of my own.' She shrugged. 'Don't worry, I think he's got the message.'

'So why are you crying?' enquired Brad irritably. 'What has he been saying to you?'

'Oh, Brad, leave it, will you?' Abby didn't

think she could take any more. 'I'll be all right. Just let me get on with my work. That's the best panacea.'

'You're sure you're up to it?'

'Heavens, yes.' Abby forced a faint smile. 'I've typed those contracts you wanted, and they're on your desk. You did want me to make a copy for Tom Halliday, didn't you?'

Brad hesitated, but without her co-operation there was nothing more he could say. He had to content himself with gaining an assurance from her that if she wanted anything—anything at all—she would let him know.

That evening she found she had had good reason for regretting her impulsive disclosure to Liz Forster. The evening paper carried an article about Rachid's impending return to Abarein, and included the information that he had been in London on a private visit, consulting his solicitors concerning a divorce from his English wife.

It was half supposition, and Abby's stomach tightened as she read the malicious comments. Obviously Liz had overlooked her behaviour at the party, and her friend's betrayal added to the weight of depression that was bearing down on her. Maybe Liz really believed that Abby's reactions were only defensive, that secretly Rachid was divorcing her because of her inability to conceive. Whatever, Abby decided bitterly that she didn't care what anybody thought, just so long as she was left alone.

Her father viewed the situation differently, however.

'How did they get to know, that's what I'd like

to hear,' he exclaimed, slapping the copy of the newspaper down on the table, and Abby quietly confessed that she had been to blame.

'Well, I'd never have thought it of Liz,' said Professor Gillespie, shocked, taking off his spectacles and polishing them on the hem of his cardigan. 'I thought she was a friend of yours.'

'So did I,' agreed Abby dryly, and took herself off to the kitchen to do the washing up.

The telephone rang later in the evening, and despite her misgivings Abby was obliged to answer it. Half afraid it might be Rachid, her response was reluctant, but it was Liz's apologetic tones that came over the wire.

'Don't tell me, I know,' she exclaimed, before Abby could say anything. 'You think I'm a heel, and you never want to see me again.'

'Something like that,' Abby responded stiffly, unwilling to be sympathetic, but Liz hurriedly tried to alter her opinion.

'It wasn't my fault—' she was beginning, when Abby interrupted her, saying flatly: 'I know, Damon forced you!' with evident disbelief. 'It wasn't like that,' Liz continued, determined to be heard, and Abby expelled her breath on a sigh as the other girl explained. 'It was Damon who wrote the story,' she insisted, the words falling over themselves in their haste to be voiced. 'But he didn't get it from me. As I hear it, he had the word from the great man himself; Prince Rachid, no less, so don't blame me for betraying your confidence.'

Abby sank down weakly on to the bench beside

the phone. 'Rachid told Damon that!' she whispered, appalled.

'Well, something like that,' Liz acknowledged compassionately, and Abby felt as if the last defence she had had been torn from her.

She was silent for so long that Liz said anxiously: 'Abby! Abby, are you still there? Are you all right?' And glad that her friend could not see her face, Abby assured her that she was fine.

'I—I'm glad it wasn't you, that's all,'· she got out at last, feeling the prick of tears behind her eyes once more. 'Look, Liz, I've got to go. The—er—Dad's waiting for some cocoa. I'll give you a ring as I promised within the next few days.'

'Okay. If you're sure you're all right. . .'

'Now that Rachid's gone home, I'll feel a lot better,' Abby promised firmly, and rang off before her uneven breathing could alert the other girl to her real reaction.

Nevertheless, in her own room, she did not try to hold back the storm of tears. There was a certain relief to be found in giving way to her feelings, and by the time she dried her eyes she felt quite purged of emotion. She almost felt up to facing Rachid himself, should he choose to come looking for her again, but she silently acknowledged it was easy to feel courageous when the opportunity to prove it was unlikely to present itself.

Work, as she had told Brad, was the best remedy. She enjoyed her job as his secretary, and perhaps because she had his sympathy, he made it easier for her to forget her problems. A trip to Ireland,

which had been planned for after Christmas, was
brought forward, and they spent ten days visiting
the refinery at Ballyvara, and staying with some
friends of his in County Wexford. The climate in
Ireland suited her, the mild, sometimes damp days
had a gentle quality about them, and Brad's
friends, the O'Malleys, were a kind and understanding couple. She didn't know what Brad had
told them about her, but they treated her more
like his girl-friend than his secretary, and she
hoped he was not beginning to get the wrong
ideas about their relationship. It would be ironic
if she had to give up her job for those reasons,
just when she needed it most.

Back in London, Christmas was beginning to
make itself felt. Although it was only November,
there were lights along Oxford Street, and all the
shops were filled with the paraphernalia of the
festive season. Children thronged, starry-eyed,
gazing at the displays in the shop windows, and
the girls in the office chattered about dances and
parties. Abby succeeded in keeping a sense of
isolation at bay only with difficulty, and she
waited for word from Rachid's solicitors with a
mixture of pain and anticipation. Until the final
steps were taken she could not relax, and she was
glad when Brad suggested she accompany him
on a trip up to Scotland, welcoming any excuse
to escape the turmoil of her emotions.

However, on the morning they were due to
depart, she awakened at six-thirty feeling absolutely terrible. She lay for a few minutes, trying
to control the nausea that was gripping her, and

then realising it was hopeless, she stumbled into the bathroom.

She was violently sick, and afterwards she leant her hot forehead against the cool tiles, praying the accompanying dizziness would leave her. But it didn't, and she eventually crawled back into bed, feeling like death.

Her father appeared at seven-thirty, after she had visited the bathroom a second time, and one look at her haggard face convinced him that she would be going nowhere that day.

'I'm sorry, my dear, but you're definitely not well enough to go flying off to Aberdeen,' he insisted gently. 'I'll telephone Daley and explain the situation. I'm sure he'll understand, and if it's imperative that you go with him, then he'll just have to postpone his visit.'

'Oh, Dad, Brad will look after me,' Abby protested, propping herself up on her elbows. 'It's just a touch of gastritis, that's all. Perhaps it was that paté I ate last night. It did have a funny taste.'

'The paté was perfectly all right. I had some myself,' retorted her father shortly. 'And in any case, you didn't eat enough to upset a fly. Come to think of it, you hardly eat enough to keep a body alive. Perhaps you should be thinking of eating more, not less, then you might not get so nauseous.'

'Food! Ugh!' Abby grimaced. 'I ache at the thought of it.'

'Well, you ought to eat something,' observed Professor Gillespie thoughtfully. 'A slice of dry toast, perhaps. Could you manage that? Then if you were sick again you wouldn't ache so much.'

Abby turned her face into the pillow. 'I'll get up—'

'I'll fetch it,' retorted her father firmly, and too weak to argue, she acquiesced.

Curiously, she felt much better after the slice of toast had been digested. So much better in fact that when her father suggested ringing Brad, she begged him to reconsider.

'Honestly, I'm sure I could go,' she pleaded, but for once Professor Gillespie was adamant.

'Maybe tomorrow,' was all he would concede, and as she had expected, Brad agreed to postpone the trip.

'He's coming round later to see how you are,' her father told her, when she came down the stairs, tying the cord of her dressing gown, and she made a gesture of resignation as she passed him on her way to the kitchen.

'There was no need,' she insisted, but Professor Gillespie ignored her, and with a shrug she helped herself to some bread from the bin.

'What are you doing?'

Her father, coming into the kitchen behind her, looked surprised, and she grinned. 'I told you I was all right,' she exclaimed. 'As a matter of fact, I feel ravenous now. That slice of toast definitely did the trick.'

'Really?'

The Professor looked thoughtful, but he made no comment, and Abby, sitting down to a poached egg a few minutes later, felt a fraud for delaying Brad over nothing more than a mirror upset.

Brad himself was all concern when he arrived in the middle of the afternoon. He brought her an enormous bouquet of winter roses, but although she was grateful for his consideration, they reminded her too poignantly of Rachid, and the time they spent together in Paris. Roses always would, she acknowledged, but she thanked Brad sincerely, and tried to apologise for her apparently speedy recovery.

'I told Dad it was nothing,' she exclaimed, fingering the petals of a creamy rose in some embarrassment. 'But he insisted on calling you, and—well, I feel a hypocrite.'

'Don't be silly.' Brad was quick to reassure her. 'There's no urgency about the trip. I suggest we give it a couple of days before we make any more arrangements. That way, you'll be sure of being completely recovered.'

'I'm recovered now,' protested Abby, but Brad was as determined as her father, and she gave in to the warm feeling of security their caring engendered.

The following morning, however, she had reason to be grateful for her father's good sense. She awakened with the same feeling of nausea, and as she sagged over the basin in the bathroom she wondered if she ought to go and see the doctor. She had no other symptoms, of course, but she had been feeling a little tired lately, and he might offer her a tonic to tone her up.

Professor Gillespie appeared as she emerged from the bathroom, and his expression was severe as he studied her pale features. 'Have you been sick again?' he asked, putting cool fingers on her forehead, and at her nod: 'How long is it going to be before you tell me?'

'Tell you? Tell you what?' Abby felt too weak for riddles. 'I don't know what it is, if that's what you're thinking. Perhaps I ought to see a doctor.'

'Perhaps you ought,' agreed her father, accompanying her into her bedroom. 'Tell me. . .' He paused for a moment, and then went on reluctantly: 'Is it Daley?'

'Is what Daley?' Abby clambered into bed, sinking back against the pillows with a feeling of helplessness. 'Dad, if you can't be more explicit, then do you mind leaving it until later. Right now, I feel too sick to care.'

'Abby!' Her father came down upon the side of the bed, taking one of her limp hands in both of his and looking at her impatiently. 'Abby, you're not a child. You must know what's wrong with you. All I want to know is, is Daley the father?'

CHAPTER SIX

'Brad!' Abby blinked, and then, as the whole weight of what her father was suggesting became apparent to her, she struggled up into a cross-legged position. 'What? What are you saying?'

'Abby, Abby. . .' Professor Gillespie tried to calm her. 'Surely you've guessed. A woman doesn't get morning sickness for no reason. Didn't it occur to you before? My God! I half suspected it yesterday, and now this seems to confirm it.'

'But I don't—I can't—that is, I can't have a child!' stammered Abby unsteadily. 'You know that. You know I can't.'

'Obviously you can,' retorted her father flatly. 'These things happen, even in the best of families.' He caught his lower lip between his teeth. 'I only wish Rachid—' He broke off abruptly. 'The sooner you get your divorce the better.'

Abby stared at him, her fingers clenching convulsively on the blankets, squeezing and unsqueezing, trying desperately to make sense of what her father was saying. But all that was beating at her brain was the unlikely possibility that she was pregnant, with Rachid's child, and for the moment that was hard enough to absorb. How long was it since she had experienced her usual bodily function? Five weeks? Six? That trip to

Ireland with Brad had thrown her out of key, and
she had had so much else on her mind, she had
not bothered to keep count of the days. Besides,
it was not something she gave much thought to
these days, and particularly not since she left
Rachid.

'I suppose it happened when you were in
Ireland,' her father was saying now, pressing his
balled fist into his palm. 'No wonder he was so
worried about you yesterday! I had my suspicions, but—'

'Dad, what are you saying?' Struggling to surface from her own bewilderment, Abby found her
father's ramblings hard to understand. 'What has
Brad to do with this? You can't imagine he and
I—' She shook her head disbelievingly. 'Dad, my
relationship with Brad is completely platonic.'

'Then who—' Comprehension dawned.
'Not—*Rachid*!'

'Of course Rachid,' exclaimed Abby crossly,
the chaotic turmoil of her thoughts temporarily
banishing the feelings of nausea. Pushing back the
covers, she swung her legs out of bed, searching
blindly for her slippers, and when she found them,
padding restlessly over to the window. 'How
could you think it was anyone else?'

Her father rose unsteadily. 'But—you seemed
so—so opposed to him when he was here. You
refused to listen to him, you behaved as if you
hated him!'

'I did. I *do*!' she got out chokingly. 'I—I
despise him—'

'Yet you're pregnant by him,' observed her

father dryly. 'Which doesn't quite add up, does it?'

Abby swung round wearily, tears trembling on the curling length of her lashes, tiny silver jewels sparkling on spears of gold. 'It was the night I went to his hotel,' she admitted, clinging to the ledge behind her for support. 'He—he took advantage of the situation, and I—and I let him.'

'Well, I'm glad you're honest, at least,' commented the Professor rather dryly. 'If you'd told me it was all his fault, I'd have found that very hard to believe. As it is, I can only abhor your recklessness in the circumstances.'

'I didn't think it would matter,' Abby muttered, bending her head. 'I mean—oh, God! How was I to know I might get pregnant? I never have before.'

Her father shrugged. 'It was always a possibility, surely you realised that.'

'No.' Abby turned her face to the wall. 'No, I didn't realise it. Dad, Rachid and I were married three years—*three years*!'

'That's not so long,' replied her father quietly. 'And towards the end you denied him your bed, didn't you?'

Abby sniffed. 'I don't want to talk about that.'

Professor Gillespie shook his head. 'I suggest we go downstairs and have some breakfast. You'll feel better after you've eaten. At least this may encourage you to eat more sensibly. You'll find your appetite will definitely improve.'

'Oh, Dad. . .' Abby turned back, resting her head against the wall behind her, her cheeks streaked with tears. 'Dad, what am I going to do? What am I going to do?'

'You're going to come downstairs and have some breakfast,' replied Professor Gillespie reasonably, 'and then we'll talk about it afterwards.'

Gathering up the dressing gown she had shed, he brought it to her, and obediently, she pushed her arms into the sleeves. But as he slipped it over her shoulders, he took a gentle hold on her, pulling her back against him for a moment and laying his cheek against her hair.

'Don't worry, my love,' he assured her gently, 'whatever happens, I'm always here. We'll work something out, never fear.'

She let him hold her for a few moments, and then she drew away, turning to put her palm against his cheek. 'Thanks, Dad,' she said, brushing away her tears with an impatient finger. 'What would I do without you?'

Her father prepared the meal, and Abby tucked in to two boiled eggs and a mountain of toast and marmalade. If anything was needed to convince her that her body was undergoing a change, the amount she ate would have done it, particularly as breakfast had never been a favourite meal. Two cups of coffee and half a slice of toast was all she had ever wanted, but suddenly she could eat generously and still feel hungry.

Nevertheless, she did feel marvellously well afterwards, and in spite of her problems there was a growing feeling of excitement inside her. She was pregnant! She was actually going to have a baby, and as she dressed she viewed her body with enlightened eyes. Was it true? Could it honestly be? Had Rachid seeded his child inside her? She felt both ecstatic and apprehensive, and unwilling to look beyond this moment to the future and all it portended.

Her father was waiting for her in the living room when she came down the stairs, and she joined him rather reluctantly, aware of what he was likely to say. Even though he had tried to reassure her upstairs, she was not unaware of his admiration for Rachid, and it was reasonable that he would expect her to tell her husband what had happened. How Rachid might react was another matter, and she crossed the room stiffly, seating herself opposite her father and viewing him with guarded eyes.

'It's just as well I don't have a tutoring session this morning,' Professor Gillespie remarked, pulling out his tobacco pouch and filling his pipe. 'I don't honestly feel up to teaching anyone today, and I wish you'd stop looking at me as if I was about to lecture you.'

Abby relaxed, and draped a jean-clad leg over the arm of her chair. 'I'm sorry. I'm tense, I suppose.'

'Not unnaturally,' observed her father, lighting his pipe. 'But not with me, I hope. I shan't try to make you do anything you don't want to do, Abby. But I have to say, Rachid will have to be told.'

Abby caught her breath. 'I suppose so.'

'There's no suppose about it,' said her father levelly. 'Naturally, first of all, we'll have to have our diagnosis confirmed, but if it's positive, and I can't see it bang otherwise, he must be informed.'

'Yes, all right.' Abby was offhand.

'That is what you want, too, isn't it?' her father enquired, looking at her over the top of his spectacles, and she moved her shoulders helplessly.

'It doesn't much matter what I want, does it?'

Professor Gillespie sighed, 'Now don't let's be silly about this, Abby. You have a responsibility to the child, whatever else is involved.'

'I know.' Abby shifted restlessly. 'I'm not arguing, am I?'

'So what do you plan to do?' her father asked, studying the bowl of his pipe. 'Will you return to Rach—'

'*No!*' Abby sprang abruptly to her feet, pacing jerkily across the floor. 'No, I won't do that.'

'Why not?'

'You ask me that?'

'Oh, Abby. . .' Professor Gillespie made a soothing gesture. 'Doesn't this shed a different light on the situation? I mean—all right, there was another woman—'

'I only know of one. There could have been others!'

'—and you feel bitter. But have you considered? If the child is a boy, he will be his father's heir?'

Abby sucked in her cheeks. 'You forget, Rachid has agreed to our divorce—'

'Abby!' Her father shook his head. 'You can hardly blame him for that.'

Abby opened her mouth to respond and then closed it again. What was the point of labouring Rachid's responsibility for what had happened?

Whatever the provocation, she had responded to his lovemaking, and even now, with the disruptive result of her recklessness destroying her hopes for the future, she was unable to deny the stirring of her senses at the memories aroused. For the first time she considered how it would be if she did return to Abarein, and the blood pounded in her ears at the prospect of living with Rachid again.

Realising her father was speaking again, she thrust these disturbing thoughts aside and concentrated on what he was saying.

'I suggest you make an appointment to see Doctor Frazer, as soon as possible,' Professor Gillespie advised her. 'Then we can decide how you're going to tell Rachid.'

'Yes.'

Abby nodded, but inside she was still less than convinced. What if it was all a ghastly mistake? she hazarded anxiously. What if she was only suffering from some awful psychological complaint, that described all the symptoms of pregnancy, without any of the substance? She had heard of cases like that. Could she conceivably have willed herself into a state of mock-pregnancy?

Even after seeing the doctor that afternoon, she found it incredibly difficult to believe what he had told her. It was like a dream, or perhaps a nightmare, she acknowledged, with all the inbuilt fears that waking up might bring. For so long she had longed for this day, but now it was here she was too stunned to feel anything but apprehension.

For the first time she allowed herself to wonder what Rachid's reaction might be. It wasn't easy to speculate on his feelings. After the way he had spoken about their divorce, it was always possible that he might deny all responsibility for it. Like her father, he already suspected Brad's affection for her, and that night at his hotel seemed such an unlikely explanation.

Then she hunched her shoulders and mentally shook herself. Who was she fooling? Whatever his faults, Rachid was not a man to shirk his responsibilities, and when he learned she was carrying his child, she doubted any force on earth would prevent him from taking what was his. He had wanted this child, just as much as she did— but for different reasons.

She returned to work the following morning, much to her father's disapproval.

'I really think you should give up your job now, Abby,' he told her brusquely the night before, but Abby was determined not to be intimidated.

'I still have my own life to lead, Dad,' she insisted firmly, and Professor Gillespie shook his head in anxious exasperation.

'What about Rachid?' he persisted, voicing the problem! Abby had been trying to avoid, and she managed to divert his tenacity only with difficulty. Eventually she succeeded in placating him by promising to write to Rachid at the weekend, but as she seated herself behind her desk that morning, she realised she might well be in Scotland by then.

Brad was delighted to see her, though he commented on her pale complexion, a hangover from

the nausea she had suffered again that morning.
'Are you sure you're well enough to be back at
work?' he asked doubtfully. 'You'll still look
very peaky. Have you seen a doctor?'

Abby hesitated. She knew she owed him
nothing less than the truth, but she was stupidly
loath to share her secret with anyone else. 'I have
seen a doctor,' she admitted now, and at Brad's
enquiring glance: 'He said it was nothing to—to
worry about. I'll be fine, honestly.'

'Well, if you're sure. . .' Brad shook his head.
'It seems to me you could do with a holiday.
You haven't looked yourself since—well, since
Rachid was here, if you must know. I think you
need a change of scene.'

'Oh, Brad!' Abby bent her head to the papers
on her desk. 'It's kind of you to care about me,
but it's really not necessary. I'm just a little under
the weather, that's all. Everyone gets a bit
depressed at this time of year.'

'What? With Christmas only weeks away?'
Brad shook his head. 'Abby stop making excuses.
You don't have to. I can guess what's wrong
with you.'

'You can?' Abby looked up at him, half in
apprehension.

'Yes.' Brad made an impatient gesture. 'It's
this divorce that's getting you down, isn't it? I
read the papers, too, you know.'

Abby gulped. 'The papers?'

'That article in the evening press, the day
Rachid was here. I saw that he wanted a divorce.
That was why he was in London, wasn't it?'

Abby closed her eyes for a moment, and then

opened them again. 'I don't think I can discuss it, Brad,' she murmured, despising her own duplicity. 'Do you mind? It—it is rather—personal.'

'Of course.' Brad was all understanding now he thought he had discovered the truth. 'Anyway, what I was about to say, regarding this fixation I have about you needing a holiday. . .' He grinned. 'How about spending Christmas with me in Mexico? The weather is ideal at this time of year, and the meetings I have to attend wouldn't take up more than half our time. We could divide our time between Mexico City and Acapulco, and we might even get to see some of those Mayan sites Bob Morris is always talking about.'

'I can't.' Abby's refusal was immediate, but she hastily qualified it by adding: 'I couldn't leave Dad at Christmas, Brad. It wouldn't be fair.'

She could also have added that the idea of leaving England at this time filled her with alarm, and she realised she wasn't going to be able to keep her condition from him for long.

'All right.' He shrugged now, obviously disappointed, but willing to make a compromise. 'After Christmas, then. We'll go in January. It will be something to look forward to while everyone here is trying to keep warn. I'll make the arrangements as soon as I can.'

Abby's head sank on to her upturned palm as soon as Brad disappeared into his own office. With her elbow propped upon the desk, she stared unseeingly through the window on to the rooftops of London. It she hadn't known better, she could almost have believed her father was at the bottom of Brad's proposition. It certainly made telling Rachid of paramount importance, unless she intended the staff to know before the child's father.

The trip to Aberdeen was postponed until the following week, and on Saturday Abby knew she had to knuckle down to writing to her husband. But what to say, and how to say it, made its composition formidable, and she was making her umpteenth attempt when the telephone rang.

Professor Gillespie was in his study, and as he didn't like to be interrupted when he was working, Abby went downstairs to answer it. But her mind was still active with the letter she had been composing, and her tone was absent as she picked up the receiver.

'Yes?'

There was an ominous crackling on the wire, and then a voice she had never expected to hear said: 'Abby? Abby, is that you?'

'*Rachid!*' she almost dropped the Biro she had been tapping against her teeth. 'I—where are you?'

'Where do you suppose?' he enquired, his voice, more real than her own voice, echoing in her ears. 'I am calling from Xanthia. I understand you wished to speak to me.'

Abby sought the padded bench, mentally berating her father for his interference. It had to be him. No one else knew of her condition, and she felt aggravated that he had not even thought to warn her.

'Abby!' Rachid spoke again, his voice mirroring his impatience. 'You did wish to speak to me, did you not? I have not been misinformed?'

'No. No. That is—' Abby moistened her dry lips. 'Oh, Rachid, I was just writing you a letter.'

'You—were writing to me?' He sounded as surprised as she might have expected. 'In what connection?' He paused. 'Ah, I comprehend.' His voice hardened. 'You have spoken to a lawyer?'

'No.' Abby was finding this twice as difficult as the written communication. 'Oh, honestly, this is very hard for me.'

'Indeed?' Rachid seemed sceptical now. 'However, as I do not know why you wished to speak with me, I am unable to help you.'

'Yes.' Abby expelled her breath on a sigh. 'I'm sorry. But I didn't expect—that is—how are you? Are you fully recovered? I expect you were glad to get home to—'

'*Abby!*' There was a grimness to his voice now. 'I did not place this call to discuss the state of my health. Nor, I hazard, did you.'

'I didn't place the call,' Abby retorted swiftly, indignation making it easier. 'My father must have asked you to ring me. I—I knew nothing about it.'

There was silence for a few seconds, and then, when she was beginning to wonder if he had rung off, he said: 'Then it is your father who wishes to speak with me? I regret—I was given the wrong message.'

'No. Oh, no.' Abby cast about desperately for the right words. 'You're right, I—I did want to—to get in contact with you. It's just—oh—'

'In the name of Mohammed, Abby, say what

must be said,' he overrode her savagely, and taking a deep breath, she faltered:

'I—I'm pregnant, Rachid. I'm going to have a baby!'

The word he used she recognised as a crude blasphemy, but she could hardly blame him. She had been shocked herself, and she at least had the physical evidence of her condition to prove it. All he had was her distant word, and the unmistakable reluctance with which she had given him the news.

'Pregnant?' he said at last, the word still a question on his tongue. Then: 'I will fly to London tomorrow. This is not something I care to discuss by any other means than a personal one.'

'Oh, but—'

Abby didn't know whether she could face Rachid so soon, nor indeed was she sure of her intentions. She needed more time to assimilate what this was going to mean to her, and she silently reprimanded her father again for precipitating the situation.

However, Rachid was not prepared to discuss it. Tomorrow,' he said, with finality in his tones, and rang off before she could say anything further.

Her father emerged from his study to find her still sitting by the phone, and he had the grace to look a little shamefaced when she raised reproachful eyes to his.

'All right, all right,' he said. 'I know what you're thinking. But I only did it for the best.'

'You should have told me,' she declared, getting to her feet rather uncertainly. 'If I'd known that it might be Rachid—'

'—you'd have refused to answer the phone,' retorted her father dryly. 'And that was why I chose not to tell you.'

Abby shook her head. 'But what did you say? Who did you speak to?'

'I don't know. Some servant or other. I didn't ask to speak to Rachid, if that's what you mean. I just left a message for him to call you, and happily, that's what he's done.'

'Happily?' Abby shivered, and walked down the hall into the kitchen, warming her cold hands on the radiator. 'He's coming to England to see me. What do you think about that? And all because you told him to ring me.'

Professor Gillespie had followed her, and now he picked up the kettle and carried it to fill at the tap. 'You must have told him about the baby,' he remarked reasonably, carrying the kettle back to the power point and plugging it in. 'I hoped you would. It's much better than writing a letter. Letters are such—impersonal things.' He turned to smile at her. 'How did he take it?'

Abby rested her back against the draining unit. 'I don't know,' she murmured uneasily. 'He was shocked, naturally, but—I don't know.'

'You did tell him that it was his, didn't you?' her father prompted briskly. 'You explained.'

'Explained?' Abby looked at him blankly. 'I—why—what was there to explain?'

'Abby!' Her father stared at her impatiently. 'For heaven's sake! You must have reminded him about that night at the hotel. Oh, lord! You didn't let him go without knowing he was the father!'

'Dad!' Abby was affronted. 'What do you think I am?'

'It's not what I think that matters,' retorted her father shortly. 'Abby, you've been asking Rachid for a divorce. What would you think, given the same circumstances?'

Abby's pale cheeks flushed with colour. 'You don't think he imagines there's someone else?'

'Why not?' Her father's tone was irritated. 'Honestly, Abby, you must have known how ambiguous a statement like that can be, particularly right now. Didn't you tell me he accused Daley of having a more than fatherly interest in you?'

Abby's shoulders sagged. 'Oh, well, if that's what he chooses to think, let him.' She moved away from the sink. 'I'm going up to my room. I feel a bit dizzy.'

'Don't you want a cup of tea?' exclaimed her father, as the kettle began to boil, but Abby shook her head.

'No, thanks,' she refused flatly, and walked wearily out of the room.

Upstairs, she flung herself on her bed, with an intense feeling of frustration. It was ridiculous to care what Rachid thought, but the fact remained, in spite of what she had told her father, she did. She felt depressed and bewildered, and dangerously near to tears, and no matter how she tried, she couldn't escape the consequences of her own foolishness.

What was she going to do? she asked herself despairingly. When Rachid came, as he surely would, what was she going to tell him? If he asked her to go back to Abarein with him, how would she respond? And ultimately, after the child was born, where did she propose to live?

It was useless to pretend that these questions would not have to be answered. Whatever happened she would be expected to hand the child over, providing Rachid believed it was his, and that would mean abandoning either her motherhood or her self-respect. But living in Xanthia meant living near Farah again, and that was something she had sworn she would never do.

CHAPTER SEVEN

ABBY spent the following day in a state of high tension. Every car door that slammed in the Mews outside brought a chill of anticipation to her spine, and when the telephone rang she froze at whatever task she was tackling, standing in numbed apprehension until her father called that it was for him.

She didn't know what time Rachid was likely to arrive. Flights from Abarein to London invariably left in the morning, but the length of the flight and the possibility of delays meant that it was impossible to correctly gauge his landing. Sunday was not the easiest day to travel, but as the afternoon drew to its close Abby felt the first pangs of troubled anxiety. What if his flight was overdue? What if it had been hijacked? The craziest notions spun round in her head so that when she served their evening meal, her appetite was practically gone.

Her father studied the untouched plate of roast beef in front of her, and laid down his own knife and fork. 'Now what's wrong?' he asked, his own concern evident, and Abby shook her head helplessly.

'It's nothing. Just apprehension, I suppose.' She glanced surreptitiously at the clock on the wall. 'Eat your dinner. Don't take any notice of me.'

126

Professor Gillespie's eyes followed hers. 'He's late, is that what you're thinking?' he suggested quietly. 'What do you want me to do? Phone the airport?'

'Heavens, no!' Abby was insistent. 'I was just checking the time, that's all. Do—er—do you think he will have eaten?'

Her father shrugged and picked up his cutlery again. 'Very probably,' he remarked. 'Either way, I can't see him sitting down to a plate of roast beef and Yorkshire pudding, can you?'

Abby fidgeted with her napkin. 'He—he used to like English food.'

'Not after a long flight,' retorted her father dryly. 'Stop worrying, Abby. I thought you'd got over that. For goodness' sake, Rachid's not an ogre. In my experience, he has always had your best interests at heart.'

'Really?' Abby was emotional. 'Even when he was with his other women, I suppose.'

'Abby, when will you realise you're not unique—'

'Do you think it makes it any easier knowing there are other women in the same situation?'

Her father sighed. 'If it hadn't been for the girl, you'd never have known anything about it.'

'Perhaps not. But I do know about her, don't I?' Abby pressed her lips tightly together, pushing the napkin aside. 'At least no one can accuse Rachid of being impotent. Who knows how many bastard children he's fathered? They may be scattered all over the Middle East!'

'Abby, you're getting hysterical! Calm yourself, and stop behaving like a foolish child!

There's more than one side to a marriage. Financially, materially, you were secure. And what was more, Rachid cared for you—'

'Oh, stop it, can't you?' Abby got up from the table, putting her hands over her ears, unwilling to listen to any more of his rationalising, and as she stood there, taut with prejudice, the doorbell rang.

Her hands fell to her sides, but neither of them moved, eventually, when the bell chimed again, it was Professor Gillespie who rose to answer it.

'Shall I?' he asked, and mutely she nodded; but she followed him to the door of the dining room, hovering there nervously while he traversed the hall.

She heard Rachid's voice as she pressed herself back out of sight against the wall. His deep attractive tones were absurdly upsetting, and she could only explain her present emotional state as a symptom of her condition. She knew a quite ridiculous feeling of embarrassment at the prospect of seeing him again, and she cast anxious eyes down over her olive silk shirt and matching corded pants, needing to assure herself of their elegant simplicity. With her hair coiled at her nape, and the plain gold chain around her neck, she looked calm and unflustered, and she prayed her inner turmoil would not expose her outer façade for what it was. As her father divested Rachid of his overcoat, she ran a probing hand over the reassuring flatness of her stomach. There was nothing to see. Apart from a slight pallor, she looked perfectly healthy, and it was still a source of amazement to her that another life was growing inside her.

She straightened as she heard her father inviting Rachid into his study, realising he would expect her to join them. It wasn't easy leaving the security of her hiding place, particularly as her nerves felt as taut as violin strings, but she had to do it, and stiffening her spine, she stepped out into the hall.

She had thought they would be already in the study, but she had forgotten Rachid's instinctive respect for his elders. He had stepped back to allow her father to precede him into the room, and as she emerged, he turned and looked at her.

Even across the shadowy width of the hall she felt the burning intensity of his gaze. With unhurried appraisal his eyes moved arrogantly over her face before dropping pointedly to her stomach, and it was all she could do not to protect herself against that significant assessment.

Then, as if his innate courtesy came to his aid, he permitted her a polite bow of his head. 'Abby,' he greeted her expressionlessly. 'Will you join us?'

'Of course.' Abby moved jerkily across the hall, but as she reached him, she allowed herself a swift examination of his lean features. Perhaps it was the muted light, but he seemed paler than was usual, his dark skin drawn tautly across his cheekbones. He seemed taller, thinner, and his mouth was drawn uncompromisingly down at the corners.

'Oh, there you are, Abby.' Her father had turned and seen her, and she quickly withdrew her gaze from Rachid and entered the study, endeavouring to appear casual as she touched his hand.

'Yes, I'm here,' she murmured, with a tight smile, and with a look of relief Professor Gillespie excused himself.

'We—er—we were just having dinner,' he explained, making a dismissive gesture. 'If you don't mind, Rachid, I'll leave you with Abby. We can talk later.'

'Oh, please—' Rachid held up his hand. 'Do finish your meal.' His eyes switched to Abby. 'Both of you. I can wait.'

'That won't be necessary,' replied Abby tersely. 'I—er—I had finished. But you go, Dad. I—we—it's all right.'

'You're sure.'

Professor Gillespie was endearingly anxious now, but Abby insisted. 'Honestly,' she nodded, hiding her apprehension, and with a shrug he left them alone.

With the closing of the door, Abby felt the now familiar sense of panic she was beginning to associate with Rachid. It was heightened by the unpleasant awareness of the censure in his expression, and she shifted rather nervously as he took up a position by the fireplace. She didn't know how to begin to explain the situation, and she pressed her balled knuckles together, as she sought for words with some meaning.

'Let us be candid, shall we?' Rachid said bleakly, before she had composed herself. 'You have told me—with evident reluctance—that you are expecting a child. Indeed, your intention was

to apprise me of that fact by letter. Do you not
think I deserved to know? And at once?'

Abby held up her head. 'What did you expect
me to do? Phone you from the doctor's surgery?
I only got to know on Tuesday myself.'

'Tuesday!' Rachid's mouth tightened. 'And
yesterday was Saturday. There are three days
unaccounted for.'

Abby sighed. 'I needed time to think——'

'Yes, I imagine you did,' he snapped harshly.
'Time to think and time to act, before I was made
cognisant of the affair. It seems to me, I should
have been the first to be told, or was it Daley
who enjoyed that doubtful privilege?'

Abby gasped. 'What do you mean?'

Rachid shook his head. 'Naturally, you do not
want the child. In the circumstances, it can only
be a source of embarrassment to you. So what
were your intentions? To dispose of it without
my knowledge?' His eyes darkened. 'You are still
my wife, Abby, in spite of the frustration that
must create.'

Abby trembled. 'Are you suggesting I would
consider——'

'Your——friend, Daley; he cannot be in favour
of losing his secretary again so soon. Even if he
is prepared to exchange a business relationship
for a marital one, when this divorce you so
eagerly seek is made absolute!'

Abby's throat felt choked. So that was what
he thought. Like her father, he had assumed the
child was Brad's, and he imagined that was why
she had been loath to tell him. She was tempted

to let him go on believing the lie, but honesty
overcame even humiliation.

'You—you have no right to criticise Brad,'
she said now, hiding her disappointment. 'He has
always been kind to me.'

'At my expense,' retorted Rachid savagely, his
lean face taut with anger. 'Without his encouragement, you would not be so opposed to reason.'

'With you?' she taunted, turning away. 'You
don't reason, you dictate!'

'*Haji*, this is impossible!' He expelled his
breath on a heavy sigh. 'Must we continually go
on in this futile way? Let us return to the reason
why I have come here. You say you are going to
have a baby. So—are you well?'

Abby sought the sofa, seating herself at the
farthest end away from him, crossing her legs and
coiling her body into the smallest space possible.
'I'm fine,' she answered, cold with disillusionment. 'I've seen a doctor, and my health is good.
I'm to visit the local ante-natal clinic after
Christmas, and—'

'What are you saying?' Rachid's fury erupted
into action. Abandoning his stiff posture on the
hearth, he strode across the room to her, standing
right in front of her, legs set aggressively apart.
'Tell me again what you just suggested. This talk
of ante-natal clinics. Are you implying that there
are no doctors in Abarein capable of attending
my wife?'

Abby shrank back against the cushions.
'You—you want me to have the baby in
Abarein?' she stammered incredulously.

'Where else would my son be born?' Rachid

grated harshly, and her lips parted.

'*Your son*?' she echoed, feeling suddenly weak. 'You believe it's your child?'

Rachid lost colour with a suddenness that left him pale and gaunt. 'Is it not?' he demanded, with an anguish that tore her apart, and she knew an almost overwhelming urge to put her arms about him.

'Yes,' she said then urgently. 'Yes, of course it's yours.' She looked up at him tremulously, ridiculously moved in spite of herself. 'I only thought—that is, my father suggested—oh, you seemed to be implying that Brad—'

'*Daley*!' He came down beside her on the couch, knees apart, hands clasped tautly between. 'Do you think I could stand here and discuss this with you if I suspected that you and Daley—' He broke off, his expression contorted with emotion. 'Dear God, Abby, what do you think I am? What kind of an opinion do you think I have of you? I trust you—I told you that.' He paused, his dark eyes probing hers. 'And I also know that no other man has touched you.'

Abby's eyes dropped before his disturbing gaze. 'You—you seemed so angry. On the phone—'

'Of course I was angry, I *am* angry,' he muttered violently. 'You do not see fit to tell me of this thing to my face. You cannot even pick up a telephone. You mean to *write* to me, a cold-blooded letter, informing me of your condition.' He shook his head. 'Even now, I do not know how you really feel.' He smote his fist into the palm of his hand. 'If only this had happened sooner! One year, two years after our marriage. Instead of waiting until it was almost too late.'

Abby's brief exhilaration in the realisation that he had not doubted her fidelity died. His words had reminded her of the real situation. It should have happened sooner, before he sought consolation with someone else, she thought bitterly, before he destroyed for ever the faith she had had in his love.

'It is too late, Rachid,' she said now, smoothing the crease of her pants, and he turned towards her, grasping her chin and tipping her face up to his.

'What do you mean?'

'You know what I mean, Rachid,' she insisted, trying to pull away from him. 'This doesn't alter anything, not really. All it means is that what should have been the end inspired a beginning. But not a beginning for us, Rachid. I've told you, that's over.'

His expression grew impatient. 'I will not accept that. Not now. Not ever.'

'No?' Her lips twisted. 'Not even when you made that statement to the *Courier* concerning your reasons for being in London last month?'

'I made no statement to the *Courier*,' he retorted, his eyes moving over her face with increasing hunger. 'Abby, Abby, listen to me—'

'If you didn't make the statement, who did?'

Rachid sighed. 'I thought you did.'

'Me?' Then: 'You read it?'

'Of course I read it. It was pointed out to me by not one but many people. Not least your friend Liz's employer, Damon Hunter.'

'And didn't you question it?'

'Did you?'

'I had no reason to.'

Yet even as she said the words, she wondered. If she had not already been vulnerable from that night spent at Rachid's hotel, she might have viewed Damon's supposition with less conviction. But she had been hurt, and she had believed it.

'You knew it was not true,' Rachid was saying now. 'I have made no attempt to gain my freedom. Why should I? It is not what I want.'

'Well, you can always marry again, can't you?' Abby derided him bitterly, fighting the attraction his nearness was evoking, but Rachid did not respond in anger.

'You know I do not follow the religion of my forefathers,' he told her, his thumb rubbing along her jawline. 'If I did, I would not permit you to live in this heathen society, that allows women to speak to their men as equals.'

'Just because I'm independent—' she began forcefully, and then choked back a gasp as his mouth touched a corner of hers. It was a tentative caress, a delicate pressure, but when his lips explored the outline of her lips, softly and sensually, before hardening over hers, weakness overwhelmed her.

'My child,' he said, against her mouth, with disruptive insistence. 'My seed inside you.' His hand spread possessively across her stomach. 'This belongs to me, Abby, and so do you. . .'

'No!'

She fought to sustain her individuality, but she was sinking beneath the wave of emotional feeling he was arousing inside her. With his hands on her body promoting an intimacy between them, and his lips searching the moist opening of hers, it was difficult to prevent herself from responding completely to him. His thigh was against hers, firm and muscular, her arm was pressed against his leg, and it would have been the easiest thing in the world to allow her instincts to lead her, and allow her hands to explore his body as he was exploring hers.

It took a superhuman effort, but at last she managed to pull herself away from him, trembling a little as she encountered the blazing passion in his eyes.

'All right,' she said, 'so you can make me want you. But it's a physical thing, a physical response, and I only hate myself afterwards.'

His cheeks drew in as if she had struck him, and without another word he got to his feet. 'You do not pull your punches, do you, Abby,' he said grimly. 'But at last I think we have got at the truth.'

Abby rose. 'We have?'

'Yes.' He turned back to her solemnly, his dark eyes rapidly losing all expression. 'You have admitted that I can arouse you, that between us there is still some spark of emotion—'

'I didn't say that.'

His eyes glittered. 'Sex, then. Is that crude enough for you? You *want* me; I want you. And I am prepared to take you on those terms.'

'Take me?' Abby stared at him. 'Take me where?'

'To Abarein, of course,' he retorted bleakly. 'We will leave at the end of the week. That should give you plenty of time to sever your association with Daley.'

'I can't do that.' Abby was obstinate. 'What you're asking is impossible.'

'Why? Why is it so? I am not asking for more than you can give. I do not expect love, Abby, only respect. Only that you should live with me until after our child is born.'

'And what then?' Abby could not deny the question, and he moved his shoulders in a dismissing gesture.

'That is up to you. As my wife, you will be free to live where you wish. But the child will stay in Abarein.'

Abby's lips moved bitterly. 'That's all you really care about, isn't it, Rachid?' she demanded. 'All this nonsense about wanting me back. . . It was a son you wanted all along. And as your wife, I'm expected to provide it. I wondered why I was being accorded so much interest. You don't like the idea of being proved wrong, and divorcing me and marrying someone else would not satisfy you, would it? Someone might suggest you were less than astute in your judgment. Why did you really come to London last month? Is Hussein angling for your position? Did your father threaten to disinherit you if you didn't produce a legitimate heir?'

She spoke cruelly and angrily, venting all her thwarted emotions in a tirade of accusation and abuse, scarcely aware of his reaction. 'But in the

name of Mohammed, I swear you will pay for
that calumny. And you will come to Abarein. You
will bear our child there. And afterwards, you can
go to hell as far as I am concerned!'

Abby came to her senses to find herself lying
on a sofa, her father's worried face suspended
above her.

'Abby, Abby, my child, are you all right?' he
was asking anxiously, and it took her several
seconds to comprehend exactly where she was
and why he should think otherwise.

Then it all came back in appalling detail. She
was still here, in her father's study, and when she
nervously twisted her head she could see Rachid's
dark-suited legs and the polished toes of his boots.
They had been arguing, she remembered. He had
torn her to pieces with the searing lash of his
tongue.

'We've been so worried about you,' Professor
Gillespie went on half reprovingly, as she lay
there feeling totally devastated. 'Fainting like
that. I've told you, you're not eating enough to
keep a fly alive!'

'When she comes to Xanthia, I will see that
she has the best of everything.' Rachid's polite
tones struck fear into Abby's tenuous conscious-
ness. 'Naturally, she will receive the finest care
available, and I myself will superintend her confinement.'

'*No!*' Abby pushed her father's fluttering hands
aside, and struggled up weakly on to her elbows.
'Dad, don't let Rachid take me away. I don't want
to leave England, I don't want to leave you—'

she choked, her throat closing up, and then to her ignominy, she burst into tears.

It was so humiliating. She had never been the type to resort to tears often, and certainly never in the company of other people. But during these last weeks, and most particularly these last days, she had found it almost impossible to control her emotions, and she sank back on the sofa now, feeling hopelessly vulnerable.

'Abby, my dear!' Her father straightened, but she saw him look at Rachid half apologetically. 'There's no need to upset yourself like this. I'm sure—*all* of us only want what's best for you. You're not well. You're tired. I told you you shouldn't have gone back to work so soon.'

'I have suggested we return to Abarein at the end of the week,' stated Rachid, moving closer to the sofa, and Abby avoided his probing gaze. 'There is no reason why my wife should not accompany me. I will have my London office attend to any details concerning her resignation from Markham Associates.'

Abby closed her eyes. 'I won't leave Brad without working my notice,' she insisted tautly. 'And I won't leave England before Christmas.'

There was silence for so long that she opened her eyes again, only to find her father exchanging a questioning glance with her husband. Rachid's face was hard and uncompromising, deep lines of impatience bracketing his mouth, while her father looked troubled and helpless, no match for the grim determination of the younger man.

'I won't,' she insisted, brushing her tears away with a careless hand. 'You can't make me,

Rachid. I—I want to spend Christmas with my father.'

'And afterwards?' Rachid demanded harshly. 'Will you then accompany me without argument? Or must I find some other method of— persuading you?'

Abby trembled. 'Blackmail, Rachid?'

'*Abby!*' Her father was shocked. 'Surely it need not come to this—this unpleasantness! You know Rachid has the right—'

'Right! *Right!*' Abby struggled into a sitting position. 'Don't talk to me about rights. What rights do I have, will someone tell me that? Or are women's rights a dirty word?'

'Abby!' Professor Gillespie turned away from her to appeal to his son-in-law. 'You see how she is. She's—not herself. This has been quite a— shock to all of us. I think perhaps it might be better if you could see your way to letting her stay with me until the new year. You're welcome to stay too, of course—'

'No, Daddy!' Abby tried unsuccessfully to control the loosening coil of her hair. Her collapse and her subsequent recovery on the sofa had dislodged the pins, and now it fell loosely about her shoulders. 'I don't want Rachid here. I want us to be alone. I—I'll go to Xanthia in January if I must, but I won't spend Christmas with him!'

'So be it.' Rachid said the words almost flatly, and Abby felt the overwhelming relief of knowing she had these few weeks of grace. 'I will come for you the first week in January. But there is one condition.'

Abby held up her head. 'Yes?'

Rachid's eyes bored into hers. 'I insist that you resign your job as Daley's secretary immediately.'

'Why should I?' Abby was indignant.

'Because that is my condition, and you know I mean what I say.'

If she had not already been the colour of a magnolia, she would have paled before the menacing threat in his tone. She had no doubt he meant what he said. All trace of emotion had been eliminated, and in its place was cold implacability, an intractable will that would suffer no opposition.

'Very well.' She submitted painfully, torn with the desire to fight him, and the knowledge that he held all the cards. Even the child she was carrying was in his control. He had that power. Power corrupts, she thought despairingly, who had said that? It was true. Rachid was enforcing his will upon her, and short of destroying the innocent life inside her, she had no means to thwart him. Even that was no solution. He could wreak some revenge on her, or if not on her, then on the people she loved or cared about. Brad, for instance. Markham Associates might not be immune from the kind of intimidation Rachid could bring to bear, and her own father was too old to face any kind of scandal.

No, she would have to go through with it. She had known that since the doctor confirmed their diagnosis. Besides, she would not do anything to harm the child, even were she given the opportunity. She would do what was demanded of her.

She would produce the heir Rachid so desperately needed. Then she would retire to some remote place where not even he could find her.

CHAPTER EIGHT

THE sun was brilliant on the blue mosaic of the tiles that surrounded the fountain. The tiles were made of lapis lazuli, and the pattern was repeated across the width of the courtyard. In the shady oasis of a fig tree Sofia, Rachid's youngest sister, sat reading her lessons, and from an adjoining court came the sound of Hussein's children splashing in the swimming pool.

From her position on a cushioned lounger set beneath the canopy of the awning, Abby fanned herself with desultory fingers. The peaceful scene should have given her pleasure, but it didn't, and she shifted restlessly as the familiar pangs of dissatisfaction came to plague her.

What was wrong with her? she asked herself impatiently. Aside from the fact that she was obliged to live here until the baby was born, why was she increasingly discontented with her lot? It should have got easier, but it didn't. It got harder, and no matter how she might wish to do so, she really couldn't blame Rachid for that!

Since her arrival almost three months ago, he had assiduously avoided her presence, and apart from a daily enquiry as to the state of her health, he left her almost completely alone. Occasionally they were required to dine with his father and the other members of the family, but mostly Abby was granted the privilege of privacy, and in consequence her time was her own.

It was not what she had expected, she realised that now. Even after that fight in her father's study, Abby had expected Rachid to demand his rights as her husband. She had thought that was to be part of her punishment in bringing her here, and in the weeks before leaving England, she had anticipated their reunion with a mixture of apprehension and excitement. Time had erased much of the fear she had felt towards him, and prolonged examination of the things she had said had convinced her she had spoken recklessly. Rachid had wanted her back, even when he assumed she could not bear him children, and she had felt a little ashamed of herself for the way she had behaved.

Of course, things had happened to relieve her feelings of guilt. Leaving Brad, for example, had left a bitter taste in her mouth, and his reactions had been typically aggressive.

'Why in God's name did you let him touch you?' he had demanded aggrievedly. 'Oh, Abby, can't you see he's going to destroy you? And you're not doing anything to stop him!'

She had understood his sense of betrayal. Twice now she had abandoned him for Rachid, and she doubted she would ever be given another chance. Despite his assertion that he would find her a job with Markhams whenever she needed it, she sensed his frustration, and she couldn't blame him for refusing her invitation to join herself and her father on Christmas Day.

Even Liz exhibited a totally uncharacteristic

display of indignation on her behalf. 'I wouldn't have had his baby!' she declared, contradicting her previous championship of Rachid's cause. 'Not when he was threatening to divorce you, I wouldn't. The man's a brute, darling. He doesn't deserve to be given a second chance!' And although Abby had attempted to explain that Rachid had not wanted the divorce, *she had*, it had all seemed a little futile. Besides, she had had the distinct suspicion that Liz didn't believe her, and as she knew about Abby visiting Rachid at his hotel, she couldn't altogether blame her.

But it was her husband's behaviour which had left her feeling so isolated and remote. Contrary to her suppositions, he had not once shown any inclination for her company, and on those rare occasions when they were together, even his polite courtesy had an edge of hostility. He had not forgiven her for what she had said, that much was obvious, and his methods of taking his revenge had proved the opposite of what she had expected. A subtle ploy, and one that was typical of him.

Perhaps it was her condition, she consoled herself, but each time Rachid left her presence with a frosty smile she felt so susceptible to his animosity, so vulnerable to these feelings of loneliness and segregation. Yet what could she expect, living in a country that was alien to her, living with his family, who had not been entirely able to hide their suspicions of her?

They must have found it strange indeed that she should have become pregnant in England. Perhaps they thought Rachid was not the child's father. All things were possible, and maybe they suspected this was a political manoeuvre, intended to remove all doubts of the succession. Abby wondered how Rachid had explained the situation to his family, but she was not appraised of his personal confidences.

Perhaps his grandmother would tell her when she returned from visiting her daughter in Egypt. Rachid's aunt Miriam was married to an Egyptian surgeon, and his grandmother had been staying with them since before Abby's arrival. She was expected home soon, though, Sofia had confided, and Abby looked forward to her coming. She had always felt comfortable with the old lady, she could talk to her, and although Nona, as she was affectionately called, had spent more than fifty years in Abarein, she still loved talking about her home in England. Perhaps she would have more compassion for her granddaughter-in-law's problems, thought Abby hopefully, as she shifted to an easier position. Surely she would understand the dilemma Abby was facing.

Hussein's wife, Yashti, had little sympathy with her sister-in-law. But then she never had. From the beginning she had resented Rachid bringing an English girl to Xanthia, and she had never tried to make a friend of her. She resented Abby, she was jealous of Rachid's infatuation with her, but perhaps it was understandable. Farah was her sister, after all.

Now Abby pushed herself up off the lounger and walked to the pillars that supported the balcony above her. Her loose smock dress was moulded to her body by her movements, the slight breeze that blew up from the ocean cooling the hot skin of her neck. In the beginning, when she and Rachid were first married, she had enjoyed living here, although she had always wished they could have had a home of their own. Nevertheless, the palace, with its many courts, was big enough to accommodate an army without their intruding on one another, and she and Rachid had had their own apartments. These apartments, actually, the ones she now occupied alone, apart from her personal servants.

Now, however, the palace had become a prison from which there was no escape. Without Rachid's company she was not allowed to leave her apartments, and the constant insulation was beginning to get on her nerves. She felt so well. She had never felt better physically. In spite of the frustration of the situation, she invariably slept as soon as her head touched the pillows, and her appetite was unaffected by her emotional upheaval. She spent her days either resting in the shade or walking in the gardens surrounding her apartments, and in consequence her limbs were soft and rounded, and her skin had acquired the golden glow of good health. She was young and she was beautiful, and without conceit, she knew that pregnancy suited her.

Supporting herself against the coolness of the pillar, she rested her cheek against her arm. Sofia, noticing her movements, had looked up from her book, and now she smiled encouragingly at her. Of all the members of Rachid's family, Sofia was the only one who had not changed towards her, and Abby was grateful for the girl's devotion.

Perhaps the fact that Sofia's mother had died just before Abby first came to Abarein had made her turn to the English girl. Whatever the reason, the twelve-year-old Sofia had been immediately attracted to her elder brother's wife, and Abby had welcomed her undemanding affections. Now, at sixteen, Sofia was approaching the fullness of womanhood, but her affections had not changed, and without her Abby would have been desolate indeed.

'It is almost time for lunch,' she said now, putting down her book and getting up from the bench she had been occupying. 'Are you hungry?'

Abby made a rueful moue with her lips and then smiled, running an exploring hand over the swelling mound of her stomach. 'A little,' she admitted. 'If I'm not careful I'm going to get as fat as Yasmin.'

'Not you.' Sofia was indignant. 'Besides, you could do with putting on a little more weight. You were quite thin when you came here.'

'I'm not thin now,' Abby pointed out dryly, and Sofia gave her a studied look.

'No, you are not,' she conceded thoughtfully. 'Having a baby obviously suits you. You are— how do you say it?—blooming!'

Abby's laughter was soft. 'Thank you. You're very kind.'

'It is true.' Sofia spoke with feeling. 'If I were Rachid—'

'But you're not,' Abby interrupted her firmly. Then: 'Have you finished your book?'

'Not yet.' Sofia accepted the reproval with good grace. 'What do I need with Homer? I am to marry Kasim. Why must I learn Latin and Greek? So long as I know how to please a man, that is the important thing, is it not?'

Abby shook her head at Sofia's deliberately outrageous statement. She knew that the girl would not dare make such remarks in either her father's or her brothers' presence, but she felt at ease with Abby, and they shared the same sense of humour.

'I imagine Kasim will expect his wife to be intelligent as well as beautiful,' Abby responded now. 'You wouldn't want him to think you hadn't a thought in your head outside your home and your children, would you?'

'Like Yashti, you mean?' Sofia suggested wickedly, coming closer to stroke her fingers down the long silvery braid of hair Abby wore over her shoulder for coolness. 'I sometimes wonder if she has ever opened a book.' She giggled. 'She certainly finds it hard to read the guilty look on Hussein's face, after he has spent a night in the *medina*!'

'*Sofia*!'

The unexpected harsh tones startled both girls, and Sofia spun round in alarm to face her elder brother. Neither of them had been aware of his entrance, his sandalled feet making little sound on the marble floor, and Abby felt her own nerves tighten as Sofia stammered her apologies.

'I—I did not know you—you were there, Rachid,' she articulated jerkily, and Abby, taking pity on her, made her own taut contribution.

'You so seldom honour us with your presence, my lord,' she taunted mockingly, and had the satisfaction of seeing Rachid's anger turn from his young sister to herself.

'Oh, Abby. . .' It was Sofia who spoke, aware of the other girl's sacrifice, but Abby only shook her head in silent admonition, and the girl took the hint and said nothing more.

'Leave us, Sofia!' Rachid commanded curtly, his eyes hard as they rested on his wife, and with a little helpless gesture she complied, leaving Abby to face her husband's wrath alone. But it was not in her nature to defy the male members of her family, particularly her father or her elder brother.

With the girl's departure, however, Abby's momentary desire for the offensive died, and self-consciously aware of how the sunlit courtyard beyond her must be outlining the swollen fullness of her abdomen, she turned abruptly into the apartment, placing herself in a less revealing position.

'To what do I owe the honour of this visit?' she enquired, endeavouring to sound casual, but Rachid was not yet ready to tell her.

'I should be grateful if you would refrain from encouraging Sofia to mock the other members of my family,' he declared coldly, prowling restlessly about the exquisitely-appointed salon. 'I know she respects you and seeks your company, and I should not care to have to forbid her to visit you here.'

'What!' Abby stared at him, irritated for once by the dark blue robes he was wearing, in deference to his father's wishes. His head was even covered by the swathe of a *kaffiyeh*, and the shadow of his beard showed on his jawline. He had never looked more alien, or more arrogant, and she felt she hated him for his unfeeling self-assurance. 'You're threatening to stop Sofia from visiting me?' she exploded. 'Oh, Rachid, do you think I'm corrupting her, is that it?'

His dark eyes were hard and unyielding as he halted in front of her. 'Perhaps,' he conceded, making the blood pound inside her head. 'You cannot deny you have no love for Yashti, but I will not permit my sister to speak disrespectfully of her elders.'

Abby sucked in her breath. 'You're afraid she'll exhibit some human instincts, aren't you?' she exclaimed tremulously. 'You're afraid that, like me, she'll show a little independence. Just because Yashti is content to live the life of a vegetable—'

'Enough!' His hand descended in a cutting gesture. 'I did not come here to discuss your opinion of my family.'

'No, I didn't suppose you did,' she countered, unwilling to be silenced like a child. 'You'll have to forgive me if my conversation is somewhat limited. Sofia is a sweet child, and I love her very much, but her chatter does tend to be rather juvenile, and naturally I cannot help but be influenced. However, as you so seldom find the time to visit this part of the palace, I suppose I should be grateful. At least she cares what happens to me. She doesn't treat me like a leper. She doesn't behave as if the sight of me disgusted her—'

She broke off abruptly at this point, realising that once again she was going too far. But she was never so conscious of her appearance as she was in Rachid's presence, and in his eyes she was sure she was fat and clumsy, and hopelessly ungainly.

The silence in the room made her apprehensive, and she cast a surreptitious glance behind her to find Rachid standing staring at her, his hands secured behind his back. It made her feel even more self-conscious, and she twisted her fingers together, wishing he would say what he had to say and go.

'I understood that you would not welcome my presence,' he said suddenly, his voice harsh and with an underlying thread of anger. 'Can you deny that you made your feelings painfully clear in London? What am I to assume from your present attitude? That your condition has mellowed your reactions to me? That cut off from all your friends and acquaintances you are desperate for anyone's company, even mine?'

'You can assume whatever you like,' she retorted, annoyed to find she was trembling. 'You can make whatever excuses you like for not visiting me, for treating me like, some shameful skeleton you'd like to keep in the cupboard. Only skeleton isn't quite the word, is it? Just the reverse. I realise I must look inelegant to you, but—'

'You are talking rubbish!' he overrode her violently, tearing the *kaffiyeh* from his head as if it irritated him. 'And you must know it. A woman with child is the fulfilment of her destiny, and no man could turn aside from his own procreation.' His voice was raw with emotion. 'You have never looked more beautiful, Abby, and I am *never* unaware of it. So do not speak to me of skeletons and cupboards. Not when I am forbidden to lay my hands on you!'

Abby quivered, aroused by his sensuous words so that she hardly knew what she was saying. 'Do you want to lay your hands on me, Rachid?' she whispered, circling her dry lips with her tongue, and she saw the way his knuckles whitened over the *kaffiyeh* in his hands.

His smouldering dark eyes bored into hers, tearing aside the gauzy threads of her defensive shield. In spite of all that had gone before, she ached for him to touch her, and her foolish expostulations melted like snow in the disruptive heat of his nearness. It was over three months since he had held her in his arms in her father's study, and shown her how weak she really was, and so much longer than that since she had known his searing possession. For whatever reason, she was remembering that now, remembering it and remembering too her own foolishness in denying that need. Right now she would have given anything to feel his hard body close to hers, and she took an involuntary step towards him, inviting his undisputed claim.

'No,' he said suddenly, his anguished voice destroying the sensuality of the moment. 'No, Abby, I do not wish to touch you.' He ran one hand round the back of his neck, massaging the muscles there as if they pained him. 'It is not my intention to promote any further contact between us, other than that which the situation demands.'

Abby fell back in dismay, her humiliation at

being repulsed compounded by the belief that his previous words had been only a sop to what he saw as her vanity. It was obvious he had really come here to undermine her friendship with Sofia, and bitterness rose like bile in the back of her throat.

'I think you'd better go,' she said, turning away to smooth her fingers over the delicate moulding of an alabaster statuette that supported a vase of thickly-petalled blossoms on its head. 'And you'd better tell Sofia, if you don't want her to visit me again. I don't see why I should do your dirty work for you.'

Her voice broke on the final syllable, and his muttered: 'Abby!' was at once angered and tormented. 'I have no desire to prevent Sofia from visiting you. On the contrary, I know she finds your companionship stimulating. I only ask that you should not condone her disobedience of my father's wishes.'

Abby bent her head, the silvery braid falling softly over the swell of her breasts. The action exposed the delicate curve of her nape, and the silky tendrils of hair that coiled there, but she was unaware of it, only conscious of her own sense of deprivation. She wished Rachid would go, before her emotions got the better of her, and although she was grateful for his indulgence so far as Sofia was concerned, she saw no reason in prolonging the interview.

However, Rachid made no move to leave her, and she had turned her head, ready to demand his departure, when he said harshly: 'I was speaking with Nona on the telephone last evening.'

'Your grandmother? Really?' Abby shrugged. 'What has that to do with me?'

'She is coming home today,' he replied, with emphasis. 'And she has asked that we—you and I—should join her for dinner this evening.' He took a deep breath. 'That is why I came. Not to spy on you and Sofia.'

Abby's nails curled into her palms. 'Of course you told her we could not.'

'No.' Rachid's voice was grim. 'I told her we should be delighted.'

'Then you'll have to make some excuse,' retorted Abby tightly. 'As you've just said, you have no wish to promote any further contact between us.'

'I added—other than the situation demands,' he countered violently. 'The present situation demands that we spend the evening together. I want your assurance that you will obey me in this.'

'*Obey you?*' Abby managed a ragged smile. 'Oh, Rachid, you do say the most tactful things!'

'I do not feel very tactful when I am with you,' he retorted, breathing heavily. 'Well? Will you come?'

Abby hesitated, but the temptation of an evening in the company of a woman she both liked and admired was irresistible.

'Very well,' she agreed, and saw the look of relief that crossed his lean face. 'I will meet you there at—what? Eight? Nine o'clock?'

'Make it eight o'clock,' he agreed, unfolding the cloth of the *kaffiyeh*. 'Until later, then.'

'*Inshallah*,' murmured Abby mockingly, and

had the satisfaction of seeing the uncertainty in his expression.

Abby dressed for the dinner appointment that evening with more enthusiasm than on any occasion since she had returned to Xanthia. She told herself it was because it was so long since she and Nona had seen one another, and she wanted to make a good impression, but deep inside her she knew a perverse desire to make Rachid regret what he had denied.

Seated before the mirror in her dressing room, she studied her complexion with critical eyes. Her skin had the honey bloom of the sun upon it, and needed little improvement, but she darkened the curling length of her lashes with mascara, and applied a subtle eye make-up that accentuated their slightly upward slant. Her mouth benefited from the application of a shiny lip lustre, and she licked her lips experimentally, liking the delicate flavour.

Leaving the mirror, she threw back the doors of her wardrobe and studied the row of clothes that confronted her. Before returning to Abarein she had equipped herself with some new clothes, suitable to both her condition and the climate, but she had to concede now that her choice had been uninspired. At the time she had felt little interest in anything, and the physical miseries of her condition had only added to her indifference. Now, however, the sickness had left her, and with it much of her apathy. There were times like now when she could even think positively, and she

sighed in impatience over the balloonlike cottons
and billowing silks.

She was still standing there, trying to decide
what to wear, when a young girl came bustling
through from the bathroom. Suni was her personal
maid, and she had been clearing up after Abby's
bath, but now she viewed her mistress's robed
figure with evident agitation.

'It is almost a quarter to eight,' she exclaimed,
in her own language, and Abby responded
likewise.

'I know it,' she said, the Arabic syllables trip-
ping easily off her tongue. 'But I cannot decide
what to wear. They are all so—tentlike!'

Suni giggled, her dark face splitting with
amusement. She was a pretty little thing, no more
than fifteen or sixteen, Abby guessed, and since
her imposed exile they had become close friends,
much to Sofia's disapproval. 'It is not suitable
that you make friends with a servant, Abby,' she
reproved her on occasion, but Abby had replied
that beggars could not be choosers, a proverb her
sister-in-law chose to ignore.

'Perhaps you could wear this,' proposed Suni
now, drawing a gown of gauzy black chiffon from
the rail, and Abby felt her nerves tighten at the
suggestion.

The gown was one she had had since before
she left Rachid. She had not taken it with
her when she made her bid for freedom, and it
had hung here, in the air-conditioned cupboard
ever since. It had held too many memories for
her to want to keep it, bought by Rachid on one
of his trips to Paris, but now she looked at it

consideringly, wondering if she could wear it.

'It is most beautiful,' Suni pressed, spreading its chiffon folds. 'And there is a fullness, here, just where it is needed, exactly as you would wish.'

Abby caught her lower lip between her teeth. 'It's not a maternity dress,' she offered half-heartedly, but Suni made light of her protests.

'You do not need the fullness of a maternity dress yet, my lady. That is why you find these other dresses so ugly. Please—try it on. See if it is suitable.'

The layers of transparent material fell softly about her, and Abby turned to her reflection with anxious eyes. The gown was cut simply, its strapless bodice veiled by a gauzy cape. Ruched chiffon was gathered beneath her breasts to fall in a thousand pleats to her ankles, and its fullness was such that it only hinted at the advancing state of her condition.

'It is perfect!' exclaimed Suni, her hands already busy at the hastily pinned coil of Abby's hair. 'And this we will leave loose, hmm? Just for this evening. I think my master will find you most beautiful.'

Abby felt the warmth of colour in her cheeks. 'I am not dressing for Prince Rachid, Suni, just for myself.'

'As you say, mistress,' Suni agreed, wielding the brush, but Abby doubted she believed her. Like all Abareinian women, Suni only saw her destiny in the service of the husband her parents would choose for her, but like all the women who lived in the palace, she was just a little in love with Prince Khalid's elder son.

It was a long time since Abby had left her hair loose, and now she viewed herself doubtfully. Pushing the heavy strands behind her ears, she half turned to look at the back, and saw that it reached her waist, a silvery cascade, straight and silky soft.

'Such a colour!' exclaimed Suni, clasping her hands in admiration. 'My lady is so lucky!'

'Am I?' Abby was sceptical, but she couldn't spoil Suni's pleasure by denying it, and with a smile she touched the younger girl's cheek.

'Thank you, Suni,' she said sincerely, and the dark girl flushed with gratitude.

To reach the Dowager Princess's apartments, Abby walked through the palace gardens, escorted by Hassan, one of the palace guard assigned to her quarters. The gardens were constantly patrolled by armed guards after dark, who kept their distance for the most part, melting into the trees when necessary to avoid intruding on anyone's privacy.

The gardens themselves were assiduously tended by a team of gardeners, and the scent of honeysuckle and verbena clung thickly to the air. Abby didn't need to see to know there were arbours of peach and apricot trees, the luscious fruit hanging within reach of an upstretched hand, and lily-splashed pools and arching fountains, whose inner illumination added to the illusion of fantasy. There were date trees and fig trees, trellises of vines and flowering creepers, and oases of greenery beside flower beds filled with every kind of blossoming shrub.

Rachid's grandmother awaited her on the terrace over-looking a sunken Italian garden. The elderly princess looked absurdly small in her fan-backed chair, bony fingers glittering with jewels curved clawlike over the arms. She was wearing a gown of crimson brocade, also glittering with sequins, but her greying eyebrows belied the tinted darkness of her upswept hair. Abby guessed she must be at least seventy, but she had hardly changed since she last saw her, and she felt a wave of reassurance when the old lady's carefully made up features relaxed into a welcoming smile.

'Abigail,' she said, ignoring the honorary title bestowed upon her grandson's wife by his father. 'Come here, child. I'm so glad you decided to come home.'

As Hassan bowed and withdrew, Abby mounted the shallow steps to the terrace, and only then did she glimpse the shadowy figure who was standing to one side of the old lady's chair. In a dark-coloured European suit, Rachid had not been immediately visible, but as she approached he moved so that the lamplight illuminated his dark features.

Abby did not look at him. She concentrated her attention on his grandmother, bending to kiss her on both cheeks in the continental fashion, drawing back so that the old lady could see her more clearly.

'You haven't changed a bit, Nona,' she said, hoping they would not notice the tremor in her voice. 'Did you have a good journey? How are Miriam and her husband? I expect they were sorry to lose you.'

'Hah, Miriam fusses too much,' declared the old lady goodhumouredly. 'She would have me get up at midday, and rest all afternoon. Too much rest hardens the arteries, that's what I told her. No matter if that husband of hers thinks he's God's gift to medicine.'

'I am sure Alex thinks no such thing,' Rachid interposed brusquely. 'He is concerned for your welfare, that is all. And you would have it no other way.'

'Hmm.' His grandmother sounded less convinced, but she allowed the topic to drop, turning instead to Abby and the coming baby. 'Come,' she said, patting the chair beside her, 'sit by me for a moment. I want to hear what's going on. Why does Rachid tell me you're staying only until the child is born? Surely this can't be true.'

Abby glanced up at her husband, and felt a disturbing thrill of satisfaction when she encountered his smouldering gaze. Obviously her appearance had surprised him, and she wondered if he remembered the dress and the memories it evoked. The temptation to find out was overwhelming, but his grandmother had asked a question and she had to answer it.

'I think perhaps—Rachid believes we are not—compatible,' she confessed innocently, hearing his sudden intake of breath at her audacity. 'He—he has his life and I have mine. After the baby's born—who knows?'

'I have never heard so much rubbish!?' Nona was shocked but still coherent. 'A child does not beget itself, Rachid. How can you talk of incompatibility with your child growing in Abigail's womb?'

Rachid's features were taut with frustration, but short of calling his wife a liar, he was obliged to suffer his grandmother's verbal castigation.

'No firm decision has been made, Grandmother,' he stated grimly, when he was allowed to get a word in. He turned burning eyes on his wife. 'Abby is a little—imaginative, due no doubt to her condition. For myself, I take full responsibility for what has happened, as you say. And so far as I am concerned, Abby is free to live here for as long as she wishes.'

'Alone?' murmured Abby, in an undertone, which she knew he could hear, and she saw his knuckles whiten before he pushed them into the pockets of his jacket.

Impatient with the conversation, Nona left her chair to lead the way into her living apartments. Following her, Abby was supremely aware of Rachid's dark gaze boring into the pale skin of her shoulders, but she endeavoured to ignore it, essaying an intense interest in her surroundings.

Like her apartments, Nona's rooms were spacious and high-ceilinged, with veined marble floors and soft jewel-coloured rugs. There were couches, but mostly her guests preferred to sit on the enormous squashy cushions that flanked a low terrazzo-tiled table. Bronze lamps cast a mellow light over dishes of nuts and sweetmeats, and the sugary confections that Abby knew from experience clung to her teeth, and in deference to Nona's nationality there was a tray containing a bottle of the dry sherry she enjoyed before dinner. Despite the household's conversion to Christianity, alcohol was still regarded with suspicion, and it was this as much as anything which added to its alien unorthodoxy.

Abby accepted a glass of sherry, and lowered herself on to the cushions. They were very comfortable, and she curled her legs beneath her, looking up at Rachid with challenging eyes. She was beginning to enjoy this game of cat-and-mouse, and after so many weeks' seclusion, she felt like a prisoner out on parole. She didn't even flinch when Rachid squatted down beside her, the velvet cuff of his dark grey jacket only inches from her shoulder as he adjusted his tie.

'You should wear black more often,' he remarked, as his grandmother seated herself on the cushions opposite, and Abby arched her dark brows.

'You bought me this dress,' she conceded softly, plucking at the material. 'I thought you might recognise it.'

'I do,' he retorted, his irises almost as black as his pupils. 'And I remember the last time you wore it, after I came back from Paris.'

'What are you talking about?' his grandmother demanded suddenly, her voice sharp with suspicion, and Rachid allowed a faint smile to lift the corners of his mouth.

'I was admiring Abby's dress, Nona,' he reassured her smoothly. 'I was telling her that she should wear black more often. Do you not agree with me?'

'I seem to remember seeing that dress before,' the old lady puzzled, with a frown. 'One like it was found by the swimming pool, wasn't it? Not so long ago. I remember your father bringing it to me, and asking if I knew whose it was.'

'Your memory is very sharp,' commented Rachid dryly, 'but condensed, I fear. There was a dress found, but it was more than three years ago.'

'Is that so?'

Nona was amazed at the passage of time, but at least her impatience with her own faltering mental powers gave Abby a breathing space. Her sudden colour would have been hard to explain, and she was relieved when Rachid switched the subject to his uncle's hospital in Cairo, and the research they were doing there. By the time Nona spoke to her again she was able to answer quite composedly, although she was aware that Rachid had not missed her heated confusion.

Dinner was a typically continental meal. Nona enjoyed French cooking, and her menus invariably favoured foods cooked in wine, and served with a variety of sauces. Abby was glad that Rachid seemed to enjoy the meal, and his reversion to European clothes made him more approachable somehow. Nevertheless, she was conscious of the guarded expression he persistently wore when he addressed her, and she guessed he had not forgotten her earlier attempts to disconcert him.

When the main course had been removed, and they were enjoying a strongly-flavoured cheese with tiny salted biscuits, Nona turned once again to the subject that was uppermost in her mind.

'When do you expect the baby, Abigail?' she asked, nodding to the servant who was serving her coffee. 'Have you seen Doctor Kemal? Is he satisfied with you?'

Abby glanced swiftly at her husband, and then answered quietly: 'I have seen Doctor Kemal, yes. And everything seems to be satisfactory. As to when I expect the baby, he estimates the end of June, about the twenty-eighth or twenty-ninth.'

'I see.' Nona snorted. Then she turned to Rachid. 'So you knew about this before I left for Miriam's.'

Rachid sighed. 'Yes.'

'And you didn't tell me?'

'I did not tell my father until the week before I brought Abby back to Xanthia,' retorted Rachid, surprising Abby herself by his statement. She had thought he would have mentioned it as soon as he returned home after visiting her. Why hadn't he? Her brows descended in a troubled frown. Had he, after all, been reluctant to do so? Or was there some other reason? Unbidden, the thought of Farah soured the rest of the evening. It was not unreasonable that he would be loath to tell his mistress of his wife's condition, and her eyes when next she looked at Rachid were filled with bitterness and resentment.

'Hmm!' Nona was still muttering over his negligence. 'It seems to me you could have confided in your grandmother. Haven't we always been friends? Haven't I always taken your part against your father, not least when you first told us about Abigail?'

Rachid's mouth drew in, and Abby could not resist the opportunity of destroying his controlled façade. 'Perhaps he had a reason for keeping it to himself, Nona,' she ventured maliciously. 'After all, it must have been very difficult for him to explain the situation to someone who had thought they had his exclusive attentions—'

'*Abby!*' Rachid's grim use of her name was dumbfounded, and even his grandmother looked a little embarrassed.

'I think this conversation has gone far enough,' she declared, pushing back her chair. 'Come, Abigail, let us talk together. I want to hear all about London, and did Rachid tell me that your mother had died? I am sorry about that. How is your father coping on his own?'

Abby allowed herself to be led away from the table, but now she didn't care that Rachid's eyes were following her. All the vitality had gone out of her, and she wished she could return to her own quarters without further humiliation.

CHAPTER NINE

IT was not late when Abby retired, Nona was
weary after her journey, and their conversation
was restrained after the things that had been said
earlier. Besides, Rachid's brooding presence was
a discouraging influence, and Abby was relieved
when Nona professed her tiredness. Refusing her
husband's stiffly proffered escort, she had the
servants summon Hassan to accompany her back
to her apartments, but once there, the whole
weight of her recklessness bore down upon her,
and she bitterly regretted her ill-mannered
indictment.

Dismissing Suni, she undressed herself, tossing
the black gown into the bottom of the wardrobe,
hoping she never had to look at it again. Then,
after sluicing her face and hands in the bathroom,
she allowed the folds of her sprigged cotton nightgown to fall about her, fastening the bootlace
shoulder straps with dejected fingers.

Part of her depression was due to the fact that
she half believed her own accusation. There had
to be a reason why Rachid had chosen to keep
her condition to himself, and the one she had
offered seemed the most logical. Somehow, living
here in seclusion, apart from the everyday hap-
penings at the palace, never hearing Farah's name
mentioned, nor encountering her simpering, flir-
tatious personality, she had almost succeeded in

forgetting the hold she had on her husband. But now the bitterness of it was back in full measure, heightened to unbearable proportions by the awareness of her own increasingly ungainly appearance. She had no defence against another woman at the moment, and she applied the brush to her hair savagely, expunging her frustration by any means she could.

Her bedroom was on the upper floor of the two-storey building. It was an attractive room furnished in the modern style, but with traditional effects like the cedarwood ottoman in the corner, and the bed itself that stood on a low dais. There were even curtains to draw about the bed when privacy was desired, but Abby had never drawn them, and she couldn't remember Rachid doing so either. The room was light, and well-proportioned, with French doors opening on to an iron-railed balcony, and the air-conditioning which had been installed throughout the palace kept all the rooms cool in high summer, and free of dust when the hot dry winds blew in from the desert.

Abby had always admired her surroundings, their classic simplicity appealing to her. The tiled floor was always cool to her toes, and the sheets on the bed were made of silk. There were matching silk curtains at the long windows, a soft shade of honey, and the plain walls were hung with jewelled paintings, reflecting an historical love for colour.

But right now Abby found nothing appealing in her surroundings. She was confused and restless, unable to relax in the cool luxury of her bed, prevented from finding oblivion by the anxious turmoil of her thoughts. For the first time, sleep did not provide an answer, and turning out all but the lamp beside her bed, she pushed open the French doors and stepped on to her balcony.

It was a beautiful night. She had never seen stars so brilliant or a sky more reminiscent of black velvet. The air too was soft, and delicately perfumed, and she could almost believe there was a heaven, and she had accidentally stumbled into it.

A shadow moved in the garden below her, and her skin prickled. It could only be a guard, of course, but nevertheless she drew back a little, unwilling that anyone should observe her so scantily attired. She guessed that if he had seen her, he would conceal himself again, but the thought that she was under observation spoiled the magic, and brought the cold realities of her situation to the forefront of her mind.

She half turned towards the bedroom, and then froze as a dark figure stepped out from the trees, on to the terrace below her. It was not one of the guards. Without exception they wore Arabian dress, whereas the intruder below her was wearing European clothes. She tried to penetrate the shadows and identify her visitor, and as she did so he called softly up to her.

'Abby! Abby, it is I, Rachid. May I come up?'

Rachid! Her mouth dried instantly, but she moved almost automatically to the rail.

'What do you want?' she whispered, aware that other eyes might still be watching them. 'I—I was just about to go to bed.'

'I want to talk to you,' he said, his hands pushed deep into his trousers pockets. 'Surely you can spare me a few minutes of your time. And before you ask, it cannot wait until morning.'

Abby caught her lower lip between her teeth. 'The servants are in bed. If I come down, I'll disturb them.'

'I know another way,' he replied, pulling his hands free and walking to the creeper that grew up to her balcony.

'You can't—that is—Rachid, it's too dangerous!' she protested, guessing his intent as he grasped the creeper and swung one leg up the wall. 'Oh, God, be careful, can't you? If the creeper breaks. . .'

'It is very strong,' Rachid assured her, as he thrust one leg over the rail and stepped on to the balcony. 'See! I am quite safe. But it is reassuring to know that you were concerned about me.'

Abby struggled to retrieve her lost dignity. 'I would have been concerned about anyone,' she retorted, suddenly aware of her state of undress. 'What on earth did you want to speak to me about that necessitates scaling the walls of your own palace?'

Rachid surveyed her very thoroughly, brushing his hands down the sleeves of his jacket, removing the creamy petals of the flowers that grew so profusely on the creeper. Then, with a polite gesture, he indicated the room behind them, and with an uneasy shrug she preceded him inside. It was obvious they could not talk on the balcony, within sight and sound of an eavesdropper, but she was reluctant to allow him access to the bedroom they had shared so intimately three years before.

With the doors to the balcony closed, Abby was supremely conscious of their isolation. She could not imagine why Rachid had come or what he had to say to her, and she pictured Suni's reaction if she was summoned to mediate between her mistress and her husband. Despite the girl's affection for her, Abby had no doubts where her real loyalties would lie, and she wrapped her arms about herself as if to ward off the very real feelings of apprehension she was experiencing.

Rachid's eyes lingered upon her, noting the nervous tightening of her lips, the way her eyes darted this way and that. But if he guessed she was alarmed by his intrusion, he made no mention of it, and instead dragged his gaze away to survey the shadowy corners of the room.

'You are comfortable here?' he enquired, after a moment, making Abby draw in her breath. 'It is little changed, you will find, but you used to like it.'

'I'm very comfortable, thank you,' Abby hastened tautly. 'But that isn't why you're here, is it, Rachid? To ask about my comfort?' She licked her dry lips. 'Would you mind coming to the point? I can guess what this is all about, and if you're about to reprimand me for speaking carelessly in front of your grandmother, then I accept that what I said was—was in bad taste.'

Rachid's mouth drew into a thin line. 'Bad taste?' he echoed dryly. 'Is that what you think? To imply to my grandmother that I am having an affair with another woman, you consider is—bad taste?'

Abby sighed, bending her head, the silky mass of her hair falling about her ears, hiding her expression. 'I suppose it was—unforgivable,' she acknowledged. Then, summoning all her strength, she lifted her head and faced him. 'But what you did was unforgivable, too, wasn't it? Am I to have no redress?'

Rachid uttered an oath. 'What is this all about? What am I supposed to have done? What—unforgivable sin am I to pay retribution for now?'

Abby hesitated. Then, squaring her shoulders, she said: 'Why didn't you tell your family I was expecting a baby? Why was it such a closely-guarded secret? Were you ashamed? Or was it, as I said, expedient for you to keep it to yourself?'

Rachid took an involuntary step towards her, and then halted, grim-faced. 'You have a suspicious mind, Abby,' he grated coldly. 'Of what possible expediency could it be to me to keep such a thing silent?'

'As I said—'

'I know what you said.' He took a deep breath. 'But contrary to your conjecture, there is no one else with a prior claim to my—how did you put it?—exclusive attentions? And my sole reason for keeping your condition to myself was a personal one.'

Abby ran a nervous hand over the gentle swell of her stomach. 'How—how personal?'

Rachid's jaw clenched. 'If you must know the truth, I was—apprehensive—'

'You? Apprehensive?' Abby almost laughed.

'Yes, I,' he snapped savagely. 'When I left you before Christmas, you were sick and desperate. How could I be sure you would not refuse to come with me when the time came? Call it pride, if you will, but I practised my deception for purely selfish reasons. Having suffered the ignominy of your repudiation once before, I hesitated to antici-pate something which might be denied me.'

Abby looked at him now, her eyes wary as she confronted his outraged indignation. Could it be true? Was that why he had kept the truth to him-self? She wanted to disbelieve him, to justify her own outburst, but his sincerity was hard to ignore.

'So no one knew?'

'No.'

'Why did you tell them you were bringing me back here, then?'

Rachid shrugged. 'I told them you had agreed to return to me. That was enough.'

'Yet you told your grandmother I would not be staying after—after the child is born.'

'Correction—I told her you had only agreed to stay until the child was born.' His eyes dark-ened. 'Do you deny this is what you said?'

Abby turned aside, caught by a trap of her own making. 'I—I—do the rest of your family know of this?'

'No.'

His response was abrupt, and she turned her head to look at him, looping her hair behind her ear as she did so. 'Why not?'

Rachid shook his head. 'Would you have me appear an object of pity? A contemptible creature worthy only of scorn? A man whose wife turns to him only as a provider, someone to supply the needs of herself and her child?'

'Your child, too, Rachid!'

'Yes, my child, too,' he agreed hoarsely, 'but only because I took advantage of you, took advantage of your compassion for a sick man, is that not what you said also?'

Abby made a negative gesture. 'You're taking my words out of context, using them against me—'

'Do you deny you only returned to me because of the child?' he demanded, stepping closer to her so that his warm breath fanned her cheek. 'Would you have returned otherwise, when no argument of mine could persuade you?'

'No. . .' admitted Abby unhappily. 'But you know—'

'I know nothing,' he retorted roughly. 'I am a man adrift on a cruel sea, tossed by tide and circumstances, defending I know not what. You say you care nothing for me, yet tonight you are all allure, all enticement in my presence. You say you despise me for what I am—well, what am I but a man, with a man's strengths and failings. You tell me you hate me, that I only want you for the child I hope you'll give me, but if that is so, why am I here now, fighting the desire to take you in my arms and administer the kind of sweet punishment only a lover can dispense?'

Abby's breathing felt suspended. 'You—you don't mean that. Not after the way you behaved this morning. You—you said you didn't even want to touch me—'

Rachid half closed his eyes against the unconscious seduction of her gently rounded figure, and Abby, watching him, felt again the unwilling stirring of her senses. She knew that if he didn't go soon, she would not have the strength to send him away, and her words were brusque as she sought to dispel the increasing intimacy between them.

'I—I think you should go,' she said, pressing her palms to the sides of her neck, moulding her hair to her nape. 'We—I—this has been quite a day, one way and another. Let's leave it now, while we're still on civil terms with one another, shall we?' She hesitated, and then added deliberately: 'If—if it's diversion you need, you'll have to look elsewhere, I'm afraid. You obviously misunderstood my—teasing. Go—go and look for Farah. I'm sure she'd be more than ready to—'

His violent imprecation cut off her words, and his narrow fingers took hold of her upper arm. He stared at her with impassioned eyes, as he struggled to contain his temper, and then, with angry emphasis, he said:

'Do you want me to go to Farah, Abby? Is that what you really want? When you forbade me your bed two years ago, was it perhaps because you were bored with that side of our marriage, and you wished to be free of an unwanted responsibility—'

Abby gasped. 'You know why—'

'Is that what you are saying now?' he persisted, ignoring her outburst. 'That even though you tremble when I touch you, you would rather avoid the inevitable conclusion to our love-play—'

'No! *No!*' Abby spoke vehemently, forgetting

for the moment exactly what she was saying in the need to defend her actions of two years before.

'No?' he taunted savagely. 'What would you have me believe? That you only kept me away from you because you were tired, because you were not well, perhaps?'

'I tell you, you know why,' she asserted tremulously. 'Can you deny that Farah was the woman your father wanted you to marry?'

'No,' he agreed, frowning, his fingers in no way loosening their hold. 'But you knew that. It is no secret. I have never denied it.'

Abby's lips trembled. 'She was your mistress, wasn't she?'

'*Haji*, you shouldn't speak of such things!' he muttered harshly. 'You are my wife. It is not seemly that we should be discussing such matters. What Farah was or was not is not in question here—'

'I disagree—'

'And I overrule your disagreement,' he retorted grimly. He shook his head a trifle wearily. 'You persist in turning over things past. Can we not consider the present? The future?'

Abby looked down at his fingers circling her arm. 'Let go of me, please. I—I'm tired. I want to go to bed. Have the decency to leave me alone.'

'So be it.'

With a heavy sigh his hand fell from her, and she covered the place it had been with protective fingers. It was always the same, she thought despairingly. They could never be together without the past rearing its ugly head, and no matter how much she might wish it were otherwise, there was no escaping the truth.

Rachid hesitated only a moment longer, and then strode towards the balcony, flinging open the doors and stepping out into the night air. Abby watched him anxiously, unwillingly aware of the sense of anticlimax his leaving always provoked. Reluctantly she acknowledged that only when she was with him did she feel truly alive, but somehow she had to overcome her weakness and face a future that had never seemed more uncertain.

Rachid swung his legs over the rail, grasping the creeper with what appeared to Abby to be careless hands. She wanted to caution him, but his eyes when she encountered them were hard and guarded, and the sardonic twist to his mouth deterred her instinctive warning. '*Saida*,' he said, inclining his head in a mocking gesture, and then Abby's cry of dismay mingled with the awful tearing sound the creeper made as it pulled free of its holding.

Rachid hurtled to the terrace below with what appeared to Abby to be devastating speed. She stood for a moment, transfixed, frozen by the horror of what had happened, and then stumbled weakly to the rail, peering down desperately into the darkness.

There was movement on the terrace, Rachid and someone else, someone who was kneeling down beside him, muttering words in stammering Arabic. Abby guessed it was the guard she had seen earlier, and turning back into her bedroom, she gathered up her muslin wrap and tied it hastily about her. Then she wrenched open her door, fleeing down the stairs which only minutes before she had denied Rachid the use of, unlocking the doors on to the terrace and emerging with tautly-strung nerves and a fast-beating heart.

'Rachid!' His name burst from her lips as she neared the two figures, faint and anguished, full of remorse for what she saw as her own selfishness. 'Oh, Rachid! Are you all right?'

The guard rose at her appearance, making the usual gesture of obeisance before indicating Rachid, who was still squatting on the mosaic tiles of the terrace, one hand supporting his head.

'Prince Rachid has suffered no serious injury, my lady,' he reassured her in his own language, the moonlight falling on her pale face, illuminating its look of concern. 'Please do not distress yourself. All is well.'

'Thank God!' murmured Abby, with heartfelt gratitude, sinking on to her knees beside her husband, touching his sleeve with unsteady fingers. 'Rachid! Rachid, are you sure you're not harmed? That was a crazy, *crazy* thing to do!'

The dark eyes were turned into her direction, and there was cynicism in their depths. 'Do not tell me you were alarmed,' he told her bitterly. 'Were I to have smashed my skull on the fountain there, you would no longer be obliged to stay with me, would you? And your friend Daley would have what he has always wanted.'

Abby stared at him unhappily. 'Don't say that, Rachid! Of course I don't wish for anything to happen to you. I—I—oh,' she shook her head, 'can you get up?'

'With a little luck,' he assayed flatly, ignoring

her outstretched hand and vaulting to his feet with more ease than she was able. 'You see, I am like the cat in your proverb. I have nine lives. I must have. You have already disposed with two of them.'

Before Abby could make any response the guard intervened.

'You are well, master?' he asked anxiously, disturbed by the bitter tone in Rachid's voice. 'You wish for me to help you back to your apartments?'

'Thank you,' inserted Abby, without waiting for her husband's response. Speaking in Arabic, she asked the guard if he would assist her in helping Rachid upstairs, and when her husband protested that these were not his apartments, she succeeded in overruling his objections by miming to the guard that he was still in a state of shock.

Apart from a slight limp, due he said to a bruised knee, Rachid had survived the fall without undue discomfort. It was remarkable really, but the distance between the balcony and the terrace was not so great, and Rachid had landed on his feet. *As usual*, thought Abby dryly, and then squashed the unworthy thought.

With the guard's departure, Rachid looked at his wife through narrowed eyes.

'Why did you do this?' he enquired, his voice taut with some emotion. 'Why could you not have allowed Rafid to take me back to my own rooms?'

Abby moved her shoulders awkwardly. 'I—I was worried about you,' she declared, aware that even to her ears it sounded thin. But then she didn't exactly know why she had asked Rafid to help Rachid upstairs, except that she had been unable to let him go without trying to make amends. 'Besides, you don't want the servants to gossip, do you? I mean, *your* falling from *my* balcony! That's certainly open to conjecture.'

Rachid expelled his breath on a weary sigh. 'And is our occupation of separate rooms not open to conjecture also? Do you not think our relationship inspires curiosity among almost everyone who lives in my father's house?'

Abby shrugged. 'I suppose it must.'

'Very well.' Rachid spread his hands. 'Then I will go—by the more conventional method this time. I will have the creeper attended to in the morning. Goodnight, Abby.'

'No! That is—wait, can't you?' Abby put out a hand towards him almost involuntarily. 'Rachid, I—I'm sorry.'

He was very stiff suddenly. 'For what are you sorry?'

Abby pressed her lips together. Even now, she couldn't forgive him everything. 'For—for making you use the creeper,' she murmured foolishly. 'I could have—I *should have* opened the door.'

'It is of no matter.' He was distant.

'Oh, but it is.' Abby couldn't help herself. She had to destroy that look of detachment he was wearing. 'Rachid, *please*! Do you forgive me?'

Without thinking, she had approached him, putting out her hand and touching his sleeve, drawing his attention to her with innocent provocation. With her hair loose about her shoulders, silvery fair where it brushed the darkness of his jacket, and her lashes still spiky from the dampness of the tears she had shed as she sped down the stairs, she was unknowingly entrancing, and Rachid, despite his stern exterior, was not unmindful of the fact.

'Go to bed, Abby,' he said thickly. 'There is nothing to forgive. I was reckless, and I paid the penalty. A hazard I have faced before, and no doubt will again.'

Abby gazed up at him reproachfully. 'You won't let me feel any better, will you?' she cried. 'You know I was to blame for what happened. Why can't we part as friends, not enemies?'

'I am not your enemy, Abby,' he insisted huskily. 'In the name of all the saints, why do you persist in tormenting me? Does it give you some kind of thrill to know what you are doing to me? Will you sleep easier knowing I shall not sleep at all?'

Abby's lips parted. 'Rachid. . .' she murmured uncertainly. 'What do you mean?'

With a groan of anguish he turned towards her, looking down into her upturned face with tortured eyes. His features were taut with emotion, and unable to prevent herself, she lifted her hand and laid it against his cheek.

Long brown fingers captured hers, turning her hand against his lips, his tongue probing its sensitive palm. Then, while she was still bemused by the breathtaking simplicity of his caress, he bent his head to her shoulder, pushing the muslin wrapper aside and exposing the delicate bones of her shoulder.

To kiss her shoulder, he had to move closer,

and his other hand slid around her thickening waist, drawing her ripening body nearer to the pulsating hardness of his. It made her overwhelmingly aware of his need of her, and while common sense urged her to break the embrace now, while she still had the chance, the throbbing magnetism he projected was a far more potent stimulant. She had been so long without the satisfying fullness of his possession, and in her over-emotional state she had little strength to fight the needs of her own body.

With the utmost gentleness Rachid swiftly divested her of the rest of her clothes, drawing in his breath as he surveyed the proud beauty of her unashamed nakedness. She was too aroused to care that earlier in the day she had denied him even the shadowy outline of her maturity, and in her quivering eagerness, she was the epitome of a woman fulfilled.

Rachid's breathing quickened as he tore off his jacket and tie, and Abby's urgent fingers sought the buttons of his shirt.

'Dear God,' he muttered, as her nails raked the arrowing of hair that grew down over his stomach, and unable to delay any longer, he swung her up into his arms and carried her to the bed.

He knew so well how to please her, she thought, as the mindless rapture of his hands upon her body invaded every corner of her mind, banishing all coherent reasoning, making her a slave to his demanding passion. She couldn't wait any longer to feel the hungry fascination of his mouth exploring hers, and when he came down

beside her on the bed, she could only wind her
arms around his neck as if she would never let
him go. She revelled in the supple hardness of
his body, in the muscled hardness of his thighs.
The sheets had never felt more sensuous against
her bare flesh, nor the warmth of the night air
more inviting against her moistening skin. This
was what she had been made for, she decided, as
Rachid's arms closed about her, arching her body
close to his, and she could only cherish the knowledge that whoever else had known his passion,
only she was capable of bringing him to this peak
of emotional frenzy. . .

CHAPTER TEN

Two weeks later Nona sent for her.

Abby had neither seen nor heard from Rachid's grandmother since that fateful night they had dined together, and although she had been troubled that she might have offended the old lady, she had had more important things to worry about.

Her most pressing concern was her reaction to her husband. No matter how she tried to deny it, her feelings towards him would not respond to sane reasoning, and not even her assertion to herself that it was her condition which was making her vulnerable could alter the fact that she no longer wanted them to be apart.

It was doubly humiliating, feeling the way she did, when Rachid obviously felt no such communication. The morning after the night he had spent in her apartments, she had awakened to find him gone, and in spite of oblique messages, sent with Suni, encouraging him to come and see her, he had remained stubbornly remote. She had eventually come to the conclusion that he regretted giving in to the urges that had governed him, and his subsequent departure for Paris four days later, on a business trip for his father, had left her feeling raw and distraught.

Nona's message came as something of an anticlimax. Abby wasn't at all sure she wanted to see the old lady, to have her probe the softened shell of her defences, and possibly expose a sensitive nerve. But messages from the Dowager Princess were treated somewhat like a royal summons, and it would have been unthinkable not to attend.

Abby dressed carefully for her interview. Her visits outside the walls of her own apartments were so few and far between, she felt she owed it to herself to put on a brave front, and her pale pink shirt and matching coral pants spurned the advancing state of her motherhood. Indeed, she looked more like a schoolgirl than her sister-in-law, as Sophia escorted her to her grandmother's apartments, and the other girl touched her hand in admiration.

'I do not know how Rachid can bear to be parted from you,' she confessed, with a heavy sigh. 'I know he can be trying at times, but I am assured he cares for you very deeply, and for the child you are carrying, of course.'

'Of course,' said Abby dryly, trying to hide the anguish Sophia's gentle words evoked. The child was all-important, she thought bitterly. Even his father had accepted that fact.

Nona was reclining on a lounger in the shade of a cluster of date palms. She looked older than when Abby had last seen her, but perhaps that was because of the dark circles around her eyes, and Abby hastened to greet her, wondering if she had been remiss in not making any contact.

'Sit down, child, sit down!' Nona's voice had luckily lost none of its strength, and Abby accepted the basket seat beside her, refusing the glass of fruit juice a smiling servant proffered.

It was pleasant in the garden at this time of day, the sun not yet reaching its zenith, and the faintest of breezes swelling in from the coast. Abby closed her eyes for a moment as the cooling draught fanned her warm cheeks, and then opened them again as Nona began to speak.

'You are well?' she asked, her sharp eyes missing nothing of Abby's appearance. 'You look disgustingly healthy, and I ask myself, why should this be so, when Rachid grows increasingly morose.'

Abby was disconcerted by the sudden attack, but she endeavoured to conceal it. 'Rachid's— disposition has nothing to do with me,' she affirmed quietly. 'As—as a matter of fact, I seldom see him.'

'No?' Nona frowned. 'He doesn't share your apartments?'

'You know he doesn't.' Abby shifted uncomfortably.

'Why not?'

'Oh, Nona. . .' With a sigh, Abby swung her feet to the ground. 'I'm sure Rachid has told you—has explained—'

'Rachid has explained nothing,' Nona retorted with impatience. 'He refuses to discuss the matter. That's why I'm forced to turn to you.'

Abby rose to her feet. 'I tried to explain, the night we came to dinner. Our—our relationship is not a—a natural one—'

'Yet you are pregnant.'

'Yes.' Abby could not deny the inconsistency.

Nona shook her head, looking every one of her seventy-odd years. 'I don't understand. How can this be? When you left here, you said it was because you could not have a child.'

Abby shrugged. 'I was wrong.'

Nona frowned. 'But why were you so certain it was you? And why leave? Rachid was shattered. You know how much he cared for you. He even went against his father's wishes in marrying you.'

'I know that.' Abby made a helpless gesture. 'Nona, you don't understand. . .'

'That's true—I don't.' The old lady fanned herself with agitated fingers. 'I gave you my support in this marriage, Abby. Surely I deserve some explanation.'

Abby sighed. 'Oh, Nona, it's not that easy. . .'

'You used to be able to talk to me.' Nona looked up at her reproachfully. 'Why is it so hard now? Are you going to tell me that you don't love Rachid any more? Is that what you find so hard to say?'

'Yes. No. Oh, I don't know. . .' Abby moved about the sunny terrace restlessly. 'I don't know what I feel any more.'

Nona's darkened brows arched. 'That's something anyway.'

'Is it?' Abby took a deep breath. 'What do you want me to tell you, Nona? I'm having Rachid's baby. Surely that must tell you something.'

'It should,' the old lady agreed. 'But it doesn't. I would like to know how it happened, but I suppose I should be accused of being inquisitive.'

Abby hesitated. 'While Rachid was in London, he—he was taken ill.'

'A touch of fever—yes, I know.' Nona nodded.

'It's a germ he picked up in the town. It recurs from time to time. I expect he told you he's been putting much time in at the hospital, teaching the children.'

'He didn't tell me.' Abby shrugged. 'Karim did. I didn't know anything about it.'

Nona nodded. 'You know how much Rachid loves children. Surely that's indirectly responsible for the present situation.'

Now Abby frowned. 'How do you mean?'

Nona spread her hands. 'You left Rachid because you couldn't give him a child, or thought you couldn't, didn't you?'

Abby felt the hot colour fill her cheeks. 'That—that was part of it, yes.'

'Part of it?' Nona sat up. 'What else could there be?'

Abby bent her head. 'I'd rather not go into that.'

'Oh, very well.' Nona was impatient, but she contained her curiosity, saying instead: 'You were telling me about Rachid being ill. Did you care for him?'

'Oh, no. At least, not exactly.' Abby sought for suitable words to describe what had happened. 'We—er—we were having dinner together, when—when he was taken ill. I helped him to bed.'

'Ah, I see.' Nona's lips twisted a little wryly. 'A case of propinquity.'

'You could say that.' Abby assented.

'So what excuse do you offer for my grandson spending the night in your apartments two weeks ago, and then taking himself off on this trip to Europe, without even saying goodbye?'

Abby's face blazed now. 'How—how do you—'

'How do I know he spent the night with you?' Nona shrugged. 'Surely you realise, after all these years, there's little that goes on in the palace without my hearing about it.' She made a moue with her lips. 'As it happens, I sent for him, later, after most of the household had gone to bed. I wanted to speak with him, to ask him—certain questions. When I discovered where he was, I decided, mistakenly, I now realise, that my questions were unnecessary. By the time I'd changed my mind, he had left for Paris.'

'Oh!' Abby linked her fingers together. 'I see.'

She was startled when Nona suddenly got to her feet, making a strangled sound of impatience. 'You love him, Abby, I know you do,' she declared irritably. 'In God's name, what is this silly game you're playing?'

Abby stepped back. 'It's no game, Nona,' she replied tremulously. 'Rachid wants an heir and, I hope, I'll provide one. That's the only reason I'm here. Anything else—anything else—is purely physical!'

'That's nonsense!' Nona was incensed. 'Don't you know Rachid loves you? Why do you persist in hurting him this way?'

'I? Hurt him?' Abby gasped. 'Nona, I can't hurt someone who's only using me!'

'Using you! What rubbish is this? Rachid is not using you—'

'Ask him,' persisted Abby, unsteadily. 'Ask

him to tell you about his other life—his other woman—'

'What other woman?' Nona was astounded.

'His woman—his mistress,' Abby choked. 'The woman who had his child! The child that proved most conclusively that Rachid was not to blame for my infertility.'

Abby didn't know how she got back to her own apartments. She felt sick and dizzy, and by the time she collapsed on the sofa in the salon, the brilliance of the sunlight was spinning about her in a kaleidoscope of colours. Her palms were moist, and a cold sweat enveloped her body, so that even in the warmth of the noonday she felt chilled to the bone.

Suni found her there approximately fifteen minutes later. The dark girl threw up her hands in horror when she saw her mistress's pale face and how the sheen of perspiration had cast an unhealthy pallor over her skin. In a whirl of flying skirts she sped for assistance, and presently cool hands assisted Abby to her feet and half walked, half carried her up the marble stairs.

In the bedroom, Suni dismissed the other servants, and herself helped Abby out of her clothes. Then, after slatting the blinds so that the sunlight fell in twilight shadows, she bathed her mistress's swearing body and drew clean cool sheets about her.

'It is the sun,' she insisted, hovering anxiously beside the bed. 'You spend too long in the sun, my lady. See how sickly it has made you feel. It can be a good friend, but a bad enemy.'

Abby forced a faint smile. 'Thank you, Suni. I'll be all right now,' she assured her, in her own language. 'If I rest for a while. . .'

'I will call Doctor Kemal,' Suni insisted, taking advantage of the familiarity they had shared. 'Prince Rachid would not forgive me if I did not take good care of you, mistress. We do not want to lose the little one, do we? Not before he has kicked his legs and blinked his eyes at the sun?'

'No, we don't want to do that,' Abby agreed flatly, turning her cheek against the pillow. 'But let me rest for a while, Suni. I—I can't see anyone now.'

In the event, Doctor Kemal arrived without being summoned. In her anticipation of seeing Rachid's grandmother, Abby had forgotten it was the day the doctor had promised to come and see her, and she suffered his exploratory examination without protest. But her pale face and the lack-lustre quality of her eyes made him hesitate before pronouncing her fit and well, and after washing his hands, he came back to the bed.

'Suni tells me you fainted this morning,' he said, speaking in English, in deference to her condition.

'Not fainted, no.' Abby moved her head weakly from side to side. 'I—just felt dizzy, that was all. It was probably the heat.'

'But the heat has never bothered you before,' he persisted, studying her strained expression. 'Tell me, Princess, are you happy here?'

'Happy?' Abby could have laughed—but it would have been an hysterical sound. 'I—I have everything I need,' she essayed slowly. 'Plenty of sunshine, good food, pleasant surroundings: why shouldn't I be happy?'

Doctor Kemal frowned. 'You answer with a question.' He hesitated. 'Do you ever leave the palace? Does your husband ever take you with him when he conducts his business dealings? Do you never go walking or driving? Are you not bored?'

'Bored?' Abby's eyes filled with tears. 'Why are you asking me these questions? What does it matter what I am? Just so long as the baby is all right.'

'Oh, your baby is most healthy, I am sure of it. He is very strong.' He smiled, laying his hand on her stomach over the silk sheet, and she felt the convulsive movement against his fingers. 'He kicks—so? You feel it? There is nothing to worry about there.'

'So what are you saying?' Abby struggled to restrain her emotion. 'The baby is all-important, isn't it?'

Doctor Kemal shook his head. 'Princess—'

'Oh, please! My name's Abby—Abigail! I'm not a princess. I'm just an ordinary working girl, who happens to be married to a man of importance.' Abby turned miserably aside from him. 'Thank you for your concern, but I'll be fine. I'm just—tired, that's all.'

Doctor Kemal had no choice but to end the interview, and for once Abby was glad of the formalities of Abareinian custom which forbade a doctor arguing with so august a patient. In England, she knew Doctor Frazer would not be so easily intimidated, and the tears she had suppressed rolled down her cheeks as a wave of homesickness swept over her.

Two things happened as a result of that conversation, however. The first was that Nona sent a car to take her driving, and the second was that Rachid arrived home three days later.

Abby was out when her husband returned. For the second time that week Nona had sent a car for her, and accompanied by Sophia, she had enjoyed a journey to Aparthos, a small village on the coast, a few miles from Xanthia.

They had walked on the beach just outside the village, and suffered the curious eyes of the traditionally-swathed peasant women, stitching the fishing nets. Sloe-eyed children stared in silent admiration at the slim blonde figure, who wore European clothes, and did not veil her hair, and Abby's stomach had plunged at the prospect of her own dark-eyed offspring. She had no doubt the baby would resemble Rachid. His was the strongest colouring, and certainly the strongest will.

The sleek limousine deposited her outside her apartments at approximately five o'clock, and bidding farewell to Sophia, Abby entered the building slowly, her eyes still dazzled by the sun. She was still a little unnerved by the emotional reaction she had had to the children, and when a tall dark figure moved into her path she was momentarily thrown into confusion. Her hands went protectively to the swelling mound beneath her camisole dress, and her breath caught in her throat as her visitor swam into focus.

'I—*Rachid*!' she exclaimed, half apprehensively. 'Wh-what are you doing here? I—I didn't know you were back.'

'I arrived only half an hour ago,' he replied formally, his voice as stiff as ever it had been. 'And where else should I be than here, greeting my wife after a prolonged period of absence? Or perhaps you have not found it so. Perhaps, after what happened, you were glad of an excuse not to see me again.'

'That's not true!' Abby could not let him think so. 'You know I wrote to you before you went away, asking you to come and see me. But you chose to ignore it.'

She brushed past him into the salon, and held her breath until she heard him coming after her. For an awful moment she thought he might take himself off again, and despite their differences she could not deny the thrill of anticipation she felt upon seeing him again.

'So?' There was a sombre note to his voice. 'I am glad to see you have recovered. When I heard you were unwell, naturally I flew home immediately.'

'Oh, I see.' Abby could not keep the bitterness out of her tone. 'Nona let you know, I suppose. Have you come home to protect your—your investment?'

Rachid's mouth tightened. 'I was concerned about you, Abby. I have been concerned about you ever since I left Xanthia.'

'Oh really?' Abby was sceptical. 'So why didn't you answer my letters?'

Rachid drew a deep breath. 'I knew this trip

was coming up. I knew I had to go away. I chose
not to face your recriminations until my return,
until I had had time to think—to plan; to find
some way to keep you in Abarein after the child
is born!'

'What?' Abby stared at him. 'Why?'

'You know why,' he declared roughly.
'Because you are my wife—and I do not wish to
let you go!'

Abby gulped. 'Rachid—'

'No.' He held up his hand. 'I will not argue
with you. I know this is not the time to do so.'
He began to massage the muscles at the back of
his neck, and then went on heavily: 'However, I
have to say I am sorry you chose to confide in
Nona, and not me.'

'To confide in Nona?' Abby's tongue circled
her dry lips. 'About—about what?'

Rachid sighed. 'Do not pretend you do not
know, Abby. Deception was never your
strong point.'

'Not like yours,' she retorted hotly, and then,
seeing the deep lines which bracketed his mouth
at her words, she hastened on: 'If you mean about
you and Farah—then I'm sure she knew already.
As you're all so fond of telling me, nothing goes
on here without everyone knowing about it!'

Rachid's shoulders sagged. 'I have told you,
Abby, I will not discuss Farah with you.'

'Then what are you talking about?' Abby's lips
trembled, and she caught the lower one between
her teeth to hide the betraying tremor. 'We
haven't talked about anything else.'

'No?' His mouth drew down at the corners.

'But she has told me that you are unhappy here, that you are apathetic and listless, and would be happier in your own country. With your father.'

Abby's lips parted now. 'I—I didn't say that,' she exclaimed. 'It—it was Doctor Kemal.' She shook her head. 'Oh, I should have known he would report back to somebody. He—he asked me if I was happy, if I ever left the palace. If I was *bored*!' She made a helpless gesture. 'What was I supposed to say? That I was esctatically happy? Hardly!'

Rachid pushed his hands deep into the pockets of his navy silk pants. He was wearing a Western suit, dark and vested, his linen as usual throwing his dark colouring into relief. He had never looked more attractive, and Abby's nerves were jumping as he paced restlessly about the salon. Why couldn't she accept him for what he was? she thought. Why couldn't she forget the past, as he wanted, and live only for the present? She had everything now, his admiration, his attention, even his love, if she could forget about Farah. She was expecting his child. Why couldn't she be content with what she had?

'So,' he said at last, coming to a halt in front of her, 'I have come to a decision. I will allow you to go to England, to be with your father, if you will promise me to come back before the child is born. It is the end of April now. I will give you five weeks. Perhaps by then we will both have learned to live with the present.'

'Oh, but—'

Abby knew an overwhelming urge to object, but Rachid was not listening to her.

'You will leave in a week's time,' he said. 'That should suffice for you to make all the necessary arrangements.'

Abby swallowed her protests. 'And—and you? What will you do?'

'I?' Rachid's expression was weary. 'I will do as I have always done, I suppose. I will attend to my father's business, and when I have some free time I will visit the children at the hospital.' He moved his shoulders dismissingly. 'What would you have me do? Come with you?'

Abby stared at him, and for a moment she knew the blind urge to say: *Yes! Yes, come with me!* But the urge passed, and with it the opportunity to turn aside the tide that was flowing against her.

The following week was filled with appointments. Appointments with the nurse, with the doctors, with the gynaecologist. She even had an appointment with a physiotherapist, and by the end of the week she was feeling more than a little weary. She felt she would have liked nothing better than to remain where she was, in the seclusion of her apartments, and the idea of returning to London, even at this most attractive time of year, did not fill her with enthusiasm. She told herself it was her condition, that she was becoming maudlin as the days progressed, but she knew it was more than that. The thought of leaving the palace, of putting thousands of miles between herself and Rachid, aroused a feeling close to panic, and she knew if he had shown the slightest desire for her to remain she would have given in eagerly.

But he didn't. He kept out of her way, and

it was left to Suni to keep her informed of his movements.

'I do not think the Prince is well,' the little maid said one afternoon, as she was brushing Abby's hair, prior to the visit of the eminent gynaecologist from the hospital, and Abby turned to her quickly.

'Not well?' she echoed. 'What do you mean— not well?' and Suni went on to explain that she had heard Rachid was not eating or sleeping, and that he spent long hours working in his study.

'I think he does not wish for you to leave Xanthia,' she confided innocently. 'I have heard that when you went away before, he refused to see anyone, even his father, for several days. And it was his brother, Prince Hussein, who eventually persuaded him that he could not remain a recluse for ever.'

'Really?' Abby tried not to reveal how intrigued she was by what Suni was saying. 'But Rachid knew I was leaving. I told him.'

Suni shrugged, and Abby acknowledged that it had not been quite that simple. The arguments they had had before she left, had created a rift between them that could not easily be bridged. And they had begun long before Abby made her final decision. Touchy and sensitive as she had been, the discovery about Farah and her child had seemed the ultimate irony, and their parting had not been amicable.

'It is such a shame,' Suni was saying now, her fingers moving rhythmically over Abby's scalp. 'You and Prince Rachid—you seem so right for one another. Now if it was Prince

Hussein—*ayi*, well, that would be different.'

Abby knew she ought not to gossip, but she had to ask the question: 'If what was Prince Hussein, Suni?'

The Arab girl coloured hotly. 'It is not for me to say, mistress,' she mumbled, turning aside to replace the brush on the dressing table, but Abby would not let her go so easily.

'No, tell me,' she insisted, and with a reluctant gesture, Suni complied.

'I only meant that Prince Hussein is not like his brother, mistress.' She hesitated. 'I do not think he would care too much if the Princess Yashti went away, do you?'

Abby shrugged. 'I hadn't thought about it.'

In truth, she did not know her brother-in-law that well. Their meetings had been confined to family gatherings, and in the early days she and Rachid had shunned too much company. Later, they had joined family dinner parties, but her association with Hussein had been limited by the overt hostility of his wife. Yashti was passionately jealous of her husband's attentions, and that was why Sophia found it so easy to mock her. Perhaps Hussein was a bit of a philanderer, perhaps he did have a mistress in the *medina*. But at least he was discreet about it, and no words of his illicit liaisons came to his wife's ears.

The subject was dropped, but Abby couldn't forget what Suni had told her. Was Rachid upset that she was leaving? Was that why he was spending long hours in his study? She lay awake at night, pondering her own reactions to his behaviour, and finding it increasingly hard to be unemotional about it. Her own feelings were so uncertain. She no longer knew what she wanted any more. Even the affair with Farah was fading into insignificance beside the persuasive thought that perhaps she had been partly to blame. If she had not believed herself to be incapable of bearing children, she might not have reacted so violently to the knowledge of her husband's infidelity, and surely there should be something in the marriage contract about forgiveness.

Nevertheless, the opportunity to see Rachid, and discover for herself how he really felt, was not presented to her. The day before she was leaving for England, she was told he had left to visit the oil refinery at Abramoud, and was not expected back until nightfall. She suspected he had gone away deliberately, to avoid any confrontation between them before she left, but she spent the day in restless seclusion, aware that somehow she had to see him before she boarded the plane. If only he was coming with her, she thought, nibbling at her nails in nervous anticipation. She needed him, she admitted it now, and if it was at all possible, she had to tell him so.

Suni informed her of Rachid's return, when she came to help her undress that night. It was late, already after eleven o'clock, but Abby had asked her to wait until the sleek limousine passed between the palace gates. If Suni wondered why her mistress wanted to know, she asked no questions, and Abby allowed herself to be disrobed with a tremulous sense of destiny weakening her knees.

The night was very dark. There was no moon,

and even the stars seemed muted in their velvet bed. But the scent of jasmine was intoxicating, and Abby's senses were stirred by its hypnotic perfume.

She waited until Suni had left her, and then, donning a cream silk robe over her high-waisted nightgown, she descended the shallow staircase. Halfway down, she was disturbed by a sudden pain in the small of her back, but guessing it was due to all the exertions she had suffered at the hands of her medical advisers, she paid it little heed. She had had various minor discomforts from time to time that day, but with so much else on her mind, she had little thought for herself.

On the terrace she hesitated, aware that she had never walked through the gardens alone at night, and that although she knew where her husband's rooms were, he could just as easily be in his study.

'Princess!'

The harsh tones of one of the guards brought her round in a whirl of confusion. But his features were gentle as he looked down at her, and she realised he could help her.

'I—I want to speak with Prince Rachid,' she averred, trying to behave as if her silken robes were her normal mode of attire. 'Do you know where he is? Can you take me to him? It is most important, or I would not be here.'

The guard looked doubtful. 'My lord the Prince has retired, my lady,' he replied gravely. 'However, I can give him a message, if you will, and maybe, if it is urgent, he will come to see you.'

'No. No, that's not what I want.' Abby tried not to sound as agitated as she felt. 'Please, I know what I'm doing. If you will escort me to the Court of the Eagles. . .'

The guard was not sufficiently familiar with Abby to argue. 'Very well, my lady,' he agreed, with a polite bow. 'If you will come this way. . .'

The soft ferns that grew along the path caressed her sandalled feet as she accompanied the guard between the espaliered fruit trees. The cry of a night bird, disturbed by their passage, was wild and eerie, and there were rustlings in the undergrowth, as the night creatures scuttled out of their way. It was late, and the palace was almost completely in darkness, except for the lamps that burned in their sconces and cast a mellow light over burnished copper shades.

Rachid's rooms seemed in darkness also, but as they approached Abby glimpsed a faint light beyond the shutters of his bedroom. Perhaps he was working, she thought hopefully, and then caught her breath as another thought occurred to her. What if he was not alone? she fretted. What if that was why the guard had been so reluctant to escort her?

'Thank you, I can make it from here,' she said now, as they reached the terrace, and the guard gave her a troubled look.

'Would you not like me to summon Prince Rachid for you, my lady?' he suggested hopefully, but Abby shook her head.

'I've told you, I can manage,' she replied firmly. 'Thank, you for your assistance. Goodnight.'

The guard shrugged, and after a moment strode away, but Abby guessed he would hover within hearing distance until he was assured she had gained entrance. Realising this, she hastily mounted the steps of the terrace and surveyed the heavy iron ring that was suspended by the panelled doors. Experience had taught her that these bells made a deafening sound and were seldom used these days. There had to be some other way of attracting Rachid's attention, and after a moment's hesitation she went back down the steps. A handful of stones should do it, she thought, looking about her impatiently, but as she bent to pick up some pebbles, another pain attacked her.

It was much more severe this time, a distinct jabbing sensation in the lower area of her spine, and she let out an involuntary cry as it caught her unawares. She straightened with some difficulty, mentally chiding herself for making such a revealing sound, and then sighed in frustration when the guard came hurrying back.

'You are ill, my lady?' he exclaimed, with much urgency. 'You cried out. What is it? Is something wrong? Did Prince Rachid not answer your call?'

'I haven't called yet,' Abby retorted, half impatiently, albeit a little troubled herself by the weakening aftermath of the pain. 'I was just about to throw a few stones at the shutters—'

The guard's instinctive reproof was silenced by another, more aggressive, tone. 'What in hell is going on here, Hassan? Have you no more sense than to argue with your woman outside my apartments?'

Abby swung round a trifle fearfully, as her

husband came striding across the terrace and down the shallow steps. He had obviously been preparing for bed, for he was wearing only a loose caftan, made of striped linen, and its open neckline exposed the bare column of his throat. Even in the shadowy light spilling from the open doorway behind him, his features looked gaunt and haggard, and his impatience with the servant was uncharacteristic of his usual courtesy. He had obviously mistaken Abby's robes for the robes of an Arab woman, but his expression changed as the breeze took the silken glory of her hair, and blew it in an aureole of silver about her head.

With a frown replacing the anger he had previously exhibited, Rachid came to an abrupt halt. 'Ah, my apologies, Hassan,' he said, as Abby took a few nervous steps towards him. 'It seems I was mistaken. I did not expect my wife to visit me this evening.'

'I regret the intrusion, my lord.'

All Hassan wanted to do was get away, and with an understanding nod, Rachid gave him his dismissal. Then, as Abby reached the steps beside him, he offered her his arm to mount them and escorted her silently inside the building.

But once inside he released her immediately, indicating the salon to one side of the wide hallway, switching on lamps to illuminate her progress.

When she had traversed half the room and come to a halt beside a low plinth on which resided a bowl of roses, he could contain himself no longer, and in low incisive tones he demanded to know why she had come.

'I thought the arrangements were all agreed,' he said, dark brows arching his irritation at the intrusion. 'You leave at ten in the morning. With luck, you should be home before dark.'

Abby drew a deep breath. 'I didn't come to see you about the arrangements, Rachid,' she averred quietly. 'That——they don't concern me.'

'What then?' He was abrupt. 'Be brief, can you? I have a long day ahead of me tomorrow.'

Abby gasped. 'You have a long day ahead of you! Do I not?'

'I am assured you did not come here to argue the length of each of our days,' Rachid replied heavily. 'Perhaps I am not very tactful. Perhaps I do not *feel* very tactful. But I am tired. Of that there is no doubt.'

Abby, still smarting from the effects of his insensitivity, was in no mood to be tactful either. 'Why is that, Rachid?' she demanded maliciously. 'I was told you weren't sleeping. I never thought to ask why!'

Rachid's face darkened ominously. 'What are you suggesting now? That I am spending my strength with *another* woman?'

Abby sniffed. 'I didn't say that——'

'You implied it.' Rachid's face was grim. 'Perhaps you think I have another woman here, at this moment? Perhaps you think that is why I am eager to get back to bed.'

Abby faltered. 'And——and have you?'

The word Rachid used was not a polite one, and his fingers as they curled about her wrist showed little mercy for the tender delicacy of her skin. Without ceremony he dragged her after him, out of the room and up the stairs, and practically pushed her into the lamplit austerity of his bedroom.

The bed was empty. It had not even been touched, and the stark simplicity of the room reflected the ascetic taste of its occupant. Only Rachid's belongings adorned the mirrored dressing table, and only his clothes lay where he had dropped them, on the jewel-coloured rug beside the bed.

'Are you satisfied now?' he demanded, in a harsh voice, raking back his hair with unsteady fingers. 'I am sorry if I hurt you, but you do not bring out the best in me, and there are times when even I cannot control my actions.'

'I know that.' Abby was feeling terrible now, not least because she guessed that Rachid thought this was why she had come—to check up on him. When it wasn't true!

'So. . .' He spread his hand. 'Now that you have satisfied yourself that I am not conducting an affair under your very nose, perhaps you will return to your apartments. I will, of course, accompany you to the airport in the morning—'

'I don't want to go, Rachid!'

The words burst from her, incapable of measured utterance, springing from her lips with all the fervency of her emotions. Whatever he had done, it was in the past. It was the present and the future that really mattered. Why had it taken her so long to see that?

If she had expected some suitable rejoinder from her husband, she was disappointed. Instead Rachid only looked at her as if he suspected some ulterior motive for her ejaculation, and his dark brows descended with brooding solemnity.

'You do not wish to go?' he said at last. 'But it is all arranged. Your father is expecting you—'

'I realise that.' Abby caught her lower lip between her teeth. 'But—but I've changed my mind. I want to stay here, with you. I want us to be together.'

To her astonishment, Rachid looked almost angry at her words. 'What is this?' he demanded, between his teeth. 'Is this some new game you are playing? Have I not danced to your tune long enough? Have you realised that while you are in England I will be free of the torment of your tantalising presence?'

'*No!*' Abby stepped towards him, but now it was he who drew back. 'Rachid, what's the matter with you? I—I thought you wanted me. You said you did. You said you loved me. Has all that changed, now that you're sending me away?'

Rachid put an unsteady hand to the back of his neck. 'I am not sending you away, Abby,' he ground out savagely. 'You wanted to go—'

'No!'

'—you told the doctor you were unhappy here—'

'No!'

'—what in God's name am I supposed to believe?'

Abby suddenly knew what she had to do. Ignoring his attempts to evade her, she came close to him, putting up her hand to his cheek and turning his face to hers.

'You can believe that I love you,' she said

huskily, as his eyes darkened incredulously. 'You can believe that I always did; even when I hated you, I loved you.'

'Abby—' He trembled as she pressed her body close to his. 'Abby, do you know what you are saying?'

She reached up to touch the corner of his mouth with her lips, her eyes answering everything he needed to know, and then, just as his hands reached for her, she experienced another searing spasm of pain. There was no mistaking its ferocity this time, and an anguished sob escaped her as she slumped in his arms.

'Abby!' His passionate protest brought her erect, and taking a trembling breath, she viewed him through misty eyes.

'Oh, darling,' she said, as comprehension gripped her, 'I think our son doesn't intend for me to go to England either. . .'

CHAPTER ELEVEN

ABBY lay in a dreamy state of contentment. She was in her own room again, or at least the room she and Rachid would share from now on. Outside, the sun was already sinking into the ocean, and soon darkness would fall, but she had no fears of the velvety advent of night. Night meant that Rachid would come to her, and even though Doctor Kemal had suggested they occupy separate rooms until Abby was recovered, she would hear none of it. She loved her husband, she needed him near her, and it was certain that nothing would keep Rachid away.

It was six hours already since she had been delivered of their son, and in spite of his precipitate arrival into the world, he had instantly made his presence felt. Despite his size—he had weighed only six pounds four ounces—he had a healthy pair of lungs, and Abby had teasingly told Rachid that he took after his father.

And in truth, he did resemble Rachid more than anyone. Even so, his hair was feather-fair, and his father had commented that he would tantalise the ladies when he grew up, with such unusual colouring.

Rachid himself had stayed with her throughout the night, and she had drawn on his strength when her own grew weak. His love had sustained her, and in her more coherent moments she had wondered how she would have coped without his boundless energy. If he was weary, he never voiced it, and his gentleness and encouragement gave her the will to succeed. She refused to allow the doctors to give her anything to ease the birth; she wanted to be totally aware of every moment. And when their son made his entry into the world, she experienced the real fulfilment of motherhood.

For Rachid, it was a wonderful moment, too. He had been so worried, so anxious, blaming himself for what had happened. He had half believed his own rough treatment of her had precipitated the crisis, and Abby had had to reassure him that she had already had warning of what was to come.

Nevertheless, the baby was premature, seven weeks premature to be precise, and no one was prepared for his arrival. Doctors were hastily summoned, nurses made their appearance, and Rachid interrogated all of them with a fervency that betrayed his inner turmoil. He was absolutely adamant that if anything should go wrong, anything at all, they were to concentrate on saving his wife before the baby. Nothing should separate them now, he told her, and if she had had any doubts that it was herself he wanted above all things, they were dramatically set at rest.

In the event, everything went smoothly. Abby gave birth without too much discomfort, and the thrill of holding her baby in her arms and of seeing the look of love and pride in Rachid's face more than made up for any pain she had suffered.

'My lady. . .'

Suni's gentle voice interrupted her reverie, and she turned bemused eyes in the girl's direction. The little maid had never been far away throughout her confinement, and she had been as enthusiastic as anyone when she first learned that her mistress had a son.

'Hello, Suni,' Abby murmured now, holding out a lazy hand, beckoning her towards the bed. 'You've seen the baby, haven't you? Don't you think he's beautiful? Don't you think he's just the most adorable baby ever?'

Suni smiled. 'He is most beautiful,' she assured her mistress eagerly, coming closer to the bed. 'Just like his mother.' She straightened the sheets. 'So—are you feeling a little less sleepy? Would you like to have a visitor?'

Abby blinked. 'A visitor?'

'It is only me, Abby,' said an elderly voice from the doorway, and as Suni moved aside Abby saw Rachid's grandmother hovering on the threshold, supporting herself on a cane.

'Nona!' she exclaimed, half propping herself up on her elbows. 'Oh, come in. Come in! Did you come to see your great-grandson?'

Nona indicated that Suni should leave them, and approached the bed slowly. Then lowering herself into a chair set close by, she said: 'Yes, I have seen my great-grandson. And admired him, as you expected.' She grimaced at Abby's indignant expression. 'Don't deny it. He's a beautiful child.'

Abby relaxed against the pillows. 'Yes, he is, isn't he?' she agreed, with some satisfaction. 'Mmm, I can hardly believe it's all over.'

Nona straightened her spine. 'Is it all over?' she enquired tautly. 'I should have thought it was just beginning.'

'Oh, it is, it is,' said Abby contentedly. 'I only meant—this time yesterday—I never dreamed—'

'No, I can believe that.' Nona studied her intently. 'I can see you feel very pleased with yourself. Why is that? Because you've given Rachid his son, or because you've gained your freedom?'

Freedom! It was a curious word for Nona to use, and Abby looked at her doubtfully. It was as if the old lady was angry with her. As if she resented the fact that Abby had had the child without her being prepared for it.

'I'm happy I've had a boy, of course,' she answered now, wondering what all this was about. 'Why shouldn't I be? It's what we both wanted.'

'Is it?' Nona's mouth was a thin line. 'Didn't you know Rachid was praying for a girl?'

'No!' Abby stared at her. 'That's not true.'

'It is true,' Nona insisted. 'I should know. He's my grandson, isn't he?'

'And he's my husband,' said Abby hotly, but Nona only waved her protests aside.

'All right,' she said. 'It seems that for Rachid's happiness I must break my word.'

'Break your word?' Abby was getting more and more confused, and Nona's words about Rachid wanting a girl didn't make any sense. She could have sworn he was delighted when she produced a son, and it hurt to think he had been deceiving her once again.

Nona sighed. 'It's about Farah,' she said heavily. 'I said I would never tell anyone what I knew, but I think the time has come.'

'Farah?' Abby felt all the strength drain from her. Not now, she thought weakly, don't tell me now, Nona, but the old lady would not have listened, even if Abby could have voiced the words.

'As you know, Farah is Yashti's sister,' Nona stated flatly. 'She is the older sister, and for a time it was expected that she and Rachid—'

'Yes, I know,' said Abby dully. 'He told me.'

'Very well.' Nona composed herself again. 'She was a frequent visitor to the palace in the old days. She and Yashti came together. Yashti and Hussein were betrothed, but it was Farah that Hussein really wanted.'

Abby's drooping lids lifted. 'Hussein?'

'Yes, Hussein,' said Nona heavily. 'Even after he and Yashti were married, he wouldn't leave her alone. Oh, maybe she was to blame. Certainly she found it hard to swallow when Rachid went off and married you. Perhaps that was what sent her off the rails. In the event, she became pregnant, and as you know, the child was born out of wedlock.'

Abby could hardly absorb what she was hearing. 'You mean—you mean—it was Hussein's child? Not Rachid's?'

'Rachid was never involved with Farah in that way,' said Nona brusquely. 'And if you had trusted him more, you would have known that for yourself. As it is, I'm forced to tell you this in a last attempt to persuade you not to leave him again. I don't know what he'll do if you do leave. I fear for his sanity—'

'I'm not leaving!' Abby had to tell her. 'Nona, I'm not leaving Rachid. I told him so last night. That was why I was with him when the baby started. I realised I no longer cared what he'd done. I love him, Nona. I love him. And I couldn't leave him, not again.'

Nona struggled to her feet. 'Abigail,' she said uncertainly. 'Child, is this true?'

Abby nodded. 'Of course it's true. I wouldn't lie about a thing like that. I was going to tell you, but when you started to tell me about Farah, I— I just couldn't get it out.'

'Oh, my dear!' Nona stepped up on to the dais, and bent to press a warm kiss to her temple. 'And here am I poking my nose into your affairs once again! I'm just an interfering old woman, and Rachid won't thank me when he learns what I've done.'

Abby shook her head. 'I can't believe it. Why didn't Rachid tell me himself? When Yashti accused him, why didn't he deny it?'

Nona sighed. 'Rachid is his father's son, Abigail. One day he'll be ruler here. How could he expose his own brother? What kind of man would do a thing like that?'

Abby was totally confused. 'But Hussein should have told the truth—'

'That's true. But Hussein is not like his brother. He will never be the man his brother is. He knows it, and I suspect Yashti knows it, too.'

'But it almost destroyed our marriage!'

'As it would most certainly have destroyed Hussein's.' Nona nodded. 'Oh, yes, Abigail, there's no doubt about that. You know how precarious that relationship is, how jealous Yashti can be.'

Abby shook her head. 'But how could Rachid be sure—'

'He couldn't. He took an enormous gamble, and almost lost.' Nona stroked her hand where it lay limply on the sheet. 'My dear, you must try to understand. Can you imagine the scandal there would have been if this had come out? As it was, it was kept within the family, and when the child died. . .' She shrugged. 'It was an act of God.'

'But where is Farah now?' persisted Abby, trying desperately to assimilate all she had learned. But all she could think of was that Rachid had borne her hatred and accusations for over two years, and his only weapon had been his love for her.

'Farah?' said Nona now, in some surprise. 'Didn't you know? I thought that was how Rachid persuaded you to come back. She married an American businessman about eighteen months ago, and now she's living in New York.'

'New York!' Abby was bemused. Then, remembering what else Nona had said, she caught the old lady's hand in hers. 'About—about the baby; what did you mean about Rachid's wanting a girl? Is that true? Did he really not want a boy?'

There were tears trembling on the tips of her lashes, and Nona touched them with a gentle finger. 'Oh, child,' she said, 'hasn't it dawned on you yet? Rachid confided in me that if you had a girl, he might be able to persuade you to stay and give him a son!'

Three months later Abby climbed out of the blue waters of a swimming pool and sauntered lazily across to where her husband was lying, watching her from a cushioned lounger. Below the gardens of this villa they had leased from a distant relative of Rachid's father, the turquoise waters of the Aegean glinted in the late afternoon sunlight, and in the distance, the vespers bell from the little Greek monastery tolled the early hour of evening.

'Come here,' commanded Rachid possessively, catching her hand and pulling her down on top of him. 'Hmm, that is better, much better,' he murmured, releasing the bra of her bikini to find her full breasts with his lips. 'Did I tell you how good it is to have you to myself again?'

'Once or twice,' responded Abby huskily, aroused as he had known she would be by his caressing lips. 'Oh, Rachid, not here, not by the pool! Anyone might see.'

'Anyone knows better than to disturb us,' he informed her masterfully, covering her mouth with his own. 'But I agree, it is not the time to make love in the open air. That is best at night.'

He moved so that Abby was half beneath him on the lounger, her slim legs imprisoned by one of his. She put up her hand and touched his mouth as he drew back, and he caught her fingers between his lips, caressing them with sensual expertise.

'You're thinking of the night you came home

from Paris, aren't you?' she whispered. 'The night I wore the chiffon gown. . .'

'. . .and we swam in the moonlight,' he agreed thickly, 'and dried one another with our bodies.'

Abby caught her breath. 'It was crazy. . .'

'It was not sensible,' he agreed softly. 'But I would do it again. Would you?'

'Oh, yes. Yes, you know I'd do anything for you,' she breathed, pressing her lips to his bare chest. 'Hmm, you smell salty. Shall we take a shower later? I promise I'll be good.'

'As you were last night?' he enquired dryly, nuzzling her ear. 'We were very late for dinner.'

'Did you mind?' she teased, knowing the answer, and his mouth sought the silky curve of her shoulder.

'To think we have two more weeks of this,' he essayed with some satisfaction. 'Do you think you can bear to be away from Robert for so long?' They had called the baby Khalid Robert, in deference to both his father and hers, but the English name was much easier to use.

'I think I might manage it,' she confessed huskily, stroking the smooth skin that covered his muscular forearm. 'And I'm sure Nona and Suni will take good care of him.'

'I pity the poor nursemaid,' agreed Rachid, with a grimace. 'My grandmother can be quite aggressive when it comes to getting her own way.'

'I know,' murmured Abby reminiscently, remembering the way she had behaved when she thought Abby was leaving, and Rachid lifted his head to look down at her quizzically.

'That was said with feeling,' he declared. 'Surely you have not been rubbing Nona—how do you say it?—the wrong way?'

Abby shook her head. 'Oh, no. It was nothing really.' She hesitated. 'She wasn't very pleased when she thought I was leaving you. She's very fond of you, you know.'

'That is how it should be,' said Rachid, with evident satisfaction, and Abby nodded her head slowly.

'She'd do anything for you, you know,' she added gently. 'Anything!'

'Including telling you about Farah,' Rachid agreed, a trifle dryly. 'Oh, yes. Do not look so apprehensive—she told me. She also told me why she told you.' He shook his head. 'How could I be angry when she had my best interests at heart?'

Abby was relieved. She hated having secrets from him. 'If only you'd told me!' she exclaimed, touching his cheek, and he bent his head to caress her temple with his lips.

'Shall I confess?' he murmured huskily. 'Shall I admit that I intended to tell you myself? If you had not changed your mind about staying after the child was born, I was going to tell you.' He sighed, shaking his head a little ruefully. 'I am not so unselfish. I am not the knight in shining armour my grandmother thinks I am. I am only a man, and I knew I could not let you go again. That was what I meant when I said I needed to think. I did. But then, when I came back, I was not even sure that my confession would make any difference. You seemed determined to go.

When Nona suggested I allow you those weeks in England—'

'Nona suggested that?'

'Yes. She said you might feel differently when you came back.'

'Oh, Rachid!' Abby wound her arms around his neck. 'I love you so much, and I've been such a fool!'

'No, I was the fool,' he insisted softly. 'But no more. From now on there will be no misunderstandings between us. You are my wife, the mother of my son, and the only woman I have ever loved. I do not think I could face life without you now.'

'Darling Rachid,' murmured Abby huskily. 'Wild horses wouldn't drive me away. . .'

MILLS & BOON®

Back by Popular Demand

Anne Mather

COLLECTOR'S EDITION

A collector's edition of favourite titles from one of Mills & Boon's best-loved romance authors.

Don't miss this wonderful collection of sought-after titles, now reissued in beautifully matching volumes and presented as one cherished collection.

Look out next month for:

Title #11	**A Haunting Compulsion**
Title #12	**Images of Love**

Available wherever Mills & Boon books are sold

MILLS & BOON®

Anne Mather

COLLECTOR'S EDITION

If you have missed any of the previously published titles in the Anne Mather Collector's Edition, you may order them by sending a cheque or postal order (please do not send cash) made payable to Harlequin Mills & Boon Ltd. for £2.99 per book plus 50p per book postage and packing. Please send your order to: Anne Mather Collector's Edition, P.O. Box 236, Croydon, Surrey, CR9 3RU (EIRE: Anne Mather Collector's Edition, P.O. Box 4546, Dublin 24).

For the spirited lover in you...

Presents™

Passionate, compelling, provocative romances you'll never want to end.

Eight brand new titles each month